SEE YOU
in the
MORNING.

MAIREAD
CASE

SEE YOU IN THE MORNING

MORNING

MAIREAD CASE

*f*eatherpr**oo***f* BOOKS

Excerpts published in: *the2ndhand, The Dil Pickler, Gesture, fnewsmagazine, Midnight Breakfast, Spolia, Two With Water,* Volume One Brooklyn's Sunday Stories, *The Unified Field,* as a *featherproof* minibook, and as a chapbook at Acephalé (Roxaboxen, Chicago IL).

Thank you, editors and organizers, and beautiful rooms of people in Chicago, New York, and Denver, and also the Ragdale Foundation, the Chicago Department of Cultural Affairs, and the Co-Prosperity Sphere, for space and time.

Published by
featherproof books
Chicago, Illinois
www.featherproof.com

First edition
10 9 8 7 6 5 4 3 2 1

Library of Congress Control Number: 2015946361
ISBN 13: 978-0983186359

Edited by Tim Kinsella.
Design by Zach Dodson.
Proofread by Ed Crouse.
Author photo by Joshua North-Shea.
Cover photo by Andrew Balet.

Printed in the United States of America
Set in Minion

for Siobhan Case

and for Rob Leitzell

"THESE ARE THE AXES: 1. BODIES ARE INHERENTLY VALID. 2. REMEMBER DEATH. 3. BE UGLY. 4. KNOW BEAUTY. 5. IT IS COMPLICATED. 6. EMPATHY. 7. CHOICE. 8. RECONSTRUCT, REIFY. 9. RESPECT, NEGOTIATE." – Mark Aguhar

"I'll find myself as I go home." – New Order

WHEN I WAS LITTLE I THOUGHT IF YOU MATCHED YOUR breath to someone else's, you would die together. For years, before Mom and Dad went out, I put my ear to Mom's ribcage and kept us safe. I didn't think about what might happen if my parents went underwater or too far away, or were hurt in an accident. I believed we'd stay in-sync because I wanted us to.

Eventually I stopped that kind of breathing, because I started listening to very slow, burnt pink music on headphones. That sludged time, which was almost as helpful. After that I forgot about our trick for years, but remembered it this summer, our last—John's and mine, Rosie's too—before we aren't high schoolers anymore.

Summer before senior year is the last time you can mess around. After that, you're applying to college or finding a job or a couple jobs or, if you're a girl, you can have a baby. You don't even need a husband to do that, though sometimes I think they make it easier. Generally though, people don't leave. If you do it's like burning a dear and expensive gift. It's ungrateful. This summer is the last one nobody really cares about. I keep wishing I could hold it, hold on to not having to make anything up so people will like me, hire me, kiss me, or whatever.

The wish stretched into dread and then a dead sadness, especially riding the bus to work at Chapters. There are all these signs on lawns, at the drugstore, in front of church. CONGRATULATIONS, GRADUATES! they yell. Why? Can't this wait? Why can't I decide when I go? Still I feel I should be appreciating it more.

I mean, I'll never win a football championship or go to war, I don't want a baby and I bet I won't get married. Who would marry me? How would it even feel? How do you look at one other person every day until you die? There is no other way to get a sign here.

On the last day of school before summer, they make all the juniors go to this coming up ceremony. If it was a fairy tale we'd be the babies in the woods without any clothes. They call the ceremony the Chrysalis. The seniors give us colored glass rings and say good luck, suckers. Parents go too, and all the cheerleaders wear their uniforms, which look like fast food restaurants or those felt pads so heavy furniture doesn't scratch the floor. The cheerleaders scream. They prance even though there isn't a game.

What I know is for sure is that I have to graduate at the end of next year, and when I graduate I have to leave because there is nobody here I want to be. Nobody. No working mirror. No synced time. Sure I like people, but I don't love them in a relaxing way. I don't love anyone like that but John, and I love him so much it makes me lonely again.

The morning of Chrysalis was warm turning warmer. If we squinted we'd smell cement and chlorine. I wore my robe. Seniors wear gold but the juniors are pylon orange, like we're circling a crime. The robes smell chemical, and they are the exact same color people wear in jail. We would be hard to lose. I put on mine before brushing my teeth, because after today they don't mean anything so I might as well look important. In the car on the way to the gym, I buffed circles on my leg. It felt like none of this was actually happening, like to make it real we should just pull over and grocery shop for the week. I wanted to buy candy bars and a plant, wearing that robe. You could probably hide whole packages of paper towels in the sleeves.

Mom kept scanning for loud songs on the radio. I couldn't see her face, but underneath the clang it sounded like she was crying, which is weird because she's the one who always talks about how my room will be for guests, once I graduate. How they will scrub my stickers off the walls. Put out a new blanket. Ever since I was little she's always said someday, you will go. It was never a suggestion. I never knew where and I don't think she did, either—just out. Gone. Oh boy, said Dad, grinning out the passenger side window. Boy! Are we proud of you!

John was already at the gym. His hair slanted to the right and his eyes had red branches in them, so he probably fell asleep in front of the TV. He does that a lot. I sat next to him in the student section and said the sign on the drugstore marquee made me teary. John said well, that's dumb. They weren't thinking about you when they put it up. I said John, that's exactly why. John and I don't actually talk that much. I think it's because we've known each other so long. I am comfortable around him.

Most moms got to the gym early to read fashion magazines or recipes while saving seats for the family. Everyone smelled clean, like they had cookies or flowers in their hair. They either looked too happy or kind of stoned. John's mom couldn't come because it was Saturday, and that's when you get good tips at the salon. But Mr. Green was there, in the back in his black shimmer shirt and favorite shoes, the ones with pilgrim buckles.

Mr. Green lives down the street from us, and once or twice a week I sit on the porch with him. I don't have to call, I just come see whether he's around. He puts out bird feeders and gets bluebirds, and we don't talk unless we want to. Sometimes we just watch the birds. When they chirp it sounds like a question.

Mr. Green comes to Chrysalis every year, even when he doesn't know the kids. He says he likes ritual, and the orange cake they put out in the church basement afterwards. You can't find that cake at any other time of year. It has tiny silver balls on top and first the icing is chewy, then so sugary your teeth hurt like chewing lightbulbs. There is caramel cake too, the kind with three milks. Mrs. Wiley-Crowe, the school secretary, makes it. Her husband is terrible and keeps telling her she should sell it. Sweetheart, it's good enough to earn us some money, but so far she always says no. Wiley-Crowe just wants to make cake for people.

I looked back and saw my parents sitting with Rosie's mom. Our moms are close. Sometimes I come home and they're on the porch together with menthols and beer, with orange slices, and they stop talking when they see me. Rosie's parents have separate bedrooms. Her dad is a famous anxious writer, and when Rosie's mom goes out, she puts her wedding ring in her pocket. When I see her at the grocery store, she always says something to show she's paying attention to me. That my shirt looks good. How did my English test go. I think she wishes Rosie and I were better friends, like that would make Rosie talk to her more too.

But Rosie floats. She doesn't really talk to anybody. Last fall though, she and John started sleeping together and that was hard because they never told me when to go home. I would just sit on the couch until I heard them moving clothes around.

Anyway, Rosie wasn't in the student seats yet. She was probably in the bathroom, lining her eyes gold or locked in a stall, folded up to eat candy someplace quiet. Sometimes Rosie just wants to be alone, which is fine because she always comes out in the end. Rosie is cooler than me because her dad is famous, but I protect her better than he does.

John's eyes were closed but he sneezed himself awake, then we sat a while and finally somebody played a horn for everyone to be quiet. We prayed in gratitude, and after that Cindy got up onstage. Cindy is a graduating senior. In the fall she's going to an out-of-state-college, and when she became valedictorian too, her dad bought her a brand-new powder-blue car. Cindy already wears the uniform for her job five years from now. Blazers, ponytail, shirts white as newly sliced apples. I am not sure why they let her talk since technically this isn't graduation.

So instead of listening to Cindy, I looked at the gym. It's the same. Everything here, everything is gold, orange, or brown. Once I fainted during the mile run, and it felt like falling into a pumpkin. Our basketball team was okay in the seventies, and the pennants are still up. If the gym was a castle, they'd be the sky above the wall at sunset. The stage is scuffed from dragging amps and chairs, the curtains are striped with duct tape, and there's a thin brown cross tacked up next to the fire alarm.

I like the crosses without Jesus on them because they are about love not sacrifice, which I guess can be about love too, but anyway. A cross without a body implies pain is not forever, and that we can focus on things other than the day he died. I mean, I know that was a big deal, but other people died that way too. When I was little I used to imagine I was a criminal in Jesus's time. I'd sit on the playground pressing wood chips into my wrists until they hurt. John used to try and poke needles all the way through his hands, but then we learned about tendons in science class and he stopped.

Being at ceremonies is the same as listening to family at holiday dinner, nodding and talking about sports without really remembering the rules, and worrying about what if my nose starts bleeding into the spaghetti pie. I would listen if school had better music or if we could stand up, or if they congratulated us for making it through, so far, without bulimia. Or without cutting anyone in the bathroom or making bad art, like where I am naked with wings for example. John understands. At least I don't think he likes it any more than I do.

Afterwards was awkward. Somebody dropped a carnation on the floor, so I picked it up and stuck the stem through the rubber bracelet on my wrist. After that I talked more gently with my hands. There were already white whiskers curling up through the petals, so I felt okay about not watering it. I kissed my parents, who kissed John too, and we all took a picture with Rosie. She came out of the bathroom with white frosted lips and was going to brunch with her mom. Rosie really likes eggs. I wasn't sure if she actually saw any of the ceremony.

After that we left. I felt sad that I never felt anything. But once we got to John's dad's really old car, which was tan and crusted in rust above each wheel, we rolled down every window and surfed the radio. John hadn't eaten anything but sour worms all day, so we got tacos from that place that sells cereal and vegetables in front. Afterwards, mouth too burned to taste anything else, I said we should take one picture, right? I think it's important to keep a record. Sometimes things make sense later.

So first I took John's picture and then he took mine. We stood in front of the menu and put our thumbs up. Mr. Green says never let anyone who doesn't love you photograph you. John's so tall his head went through the A in TACOS! Do you feel different? he asked, and I said maybe. I don't know yet.

This city is small enough to walk across in one morning. I've lived here my whole life. There's a muffin bar at the grocery store. They have different flavors different days, like chocolate chocolate or poppyseed or pistachio green, and they glaze half of each batch like cold on windows. There is turkey gravy on the fish special at the diner on Fridays, and ceramic geese in hats on porches. There are shivery deep-black lines when hills crest on long roads in the summer. Everyone played soccer with mean girls, and boys who didn't want to look gay. Everyone's mom has pink wine in a box in the fridge. There are crocheted tissue-box holders and seashell soaps nobody actually uses, and tiny mysterious towels patterned in shamrocks or hearts, or pink ribbons against breast cancer. There are family rooms and living rooms. Once every few years, someone has a bad accident on icy roads, and afterwards there is a campaign to raise awareness.

Pretty much everyone is Catholic. I am too, I guess, I mean I've never been anything else, and Mom is. John's mom isn't, after her divorce, but he goes to Mass with me sometimes. It's the only place he's ever been where that many people hold hands. John doesn't take the bread. He just kneels and bows his head while the rest of us go up. Once I saw his lips moving, so I asked if he prayed. No, he said. Duh, he was reciting lyrics.

Our neighbors' yard has two crosses and an American flag, and fake pastel children hiding their faces in shame, and in the trees, little yellow ribbons. In the springtime, the husband does this Graveyard of the Unborn. He sticks plywood crosses in the grass, popping them up like Whac-a-Mole all the way to the mailbox. I didn't know why so I asked, and he said it was for all the dead babies. Each cross, he said, trees budding fists behind him, represents three babies, and our yard is one day in this country. He scared me because okay, nobody believes everything the same all the time, but a yard full of crosses is like a burning house. You can't argue with it. There isn't time for questions either.

A couple years ago in English class, Troy P. said what if every character in a book is also the soul of a dead baby? What if that's why literature is so beautiful and real? I knew he was trying to work it out, so instead of shaking him I rubbed a pink eraser to crumbs in my lap.

When John got her pregnant, we took Rosie to the clinic. Well, I mean when they got each other pregnant. Afterwards Rosie slept twelve hours, and every hour I held a mirror in front of her mouth to make sure she wasn't dead. When she woke up, we all got pancakes and anyway, it was fine. I was just glad we all got home. Rosie said it didn't really hurt. Sometimes she dreams about this little marshmallow elephant. She thinks it's her baby's ghost saying he got home safe too.

John and I both have jobs. Rosie doesn't. She doesn't have to, which is fine only I would be bored. John works at Starlite Jams, a theme restaurant where kids spend quarters tickets to play inflate-a-basketball or roller skate for fifteen minutes, and afterwards they win finger traps and glitter-rubber balls.

On the way out there is a basket of hard sweet fruit candy for the kids who didn't get a prize. It's kept under a light, so all the candy and the plastic wrappers heat up and glob together. Two of the lemons have been on top since John and I went skating there ourselves.

John works twenty hours a week, on the weekends mostly. Usually he just walks around in a rabbit costume, but sometimes he heats up pizzas and makes shaved ice rainbow. He serves the dry, fruit, and hot ice cream toppings so little kids don't overdo it. Plus most of them are too short to see their options in the bins anyway, but they'll tell the rabbit what they want. Sometimes John breaks up fights, because kids listen to a rabbit. The fur is brown, and the ears are twice as long as John's shins. If ice cream gets in your pelt, they take it from your pay. John says the crotch smells awful, and I asked why he smelled it in the first place.

John would be a rabbit forever if they'd let him. He wants to stay in town and work, and buy a house someday. Kids and a dog, or whatever. He doesn't want to go to college and he doesn't want to leave his mom. But I think if I stayed it'd be like shaving off my hair. My face would start to look mean. So maybe we could try leaving here together. I'd promise John to help.

For now I work at Chapters, a big box bookstore. It used to be a bowling alley, so everything feels thrown-out and stretched long. Sometimes old people come in and say oh ho, I used to bowl here, and I say wow, I bet so. That's great. Two of them came in wearing matching turquoise jogging suits with roses printed up and down the arms. They were holding hands and said they fell in love here, bowling. I guess he rolled a turkey, and she was somebody's little sister. When they kissed she closed her eyes, and I saw her eyeshadow matched their turquoise. They must wear those suits a lot.

Sometimes people come here around dates, as a safe place to meet before the movie starts or something. They will touch each other's elbows or talk about weather patterns, or be too careful about books they obviously love a lot. Usually I ask where they met and whether they're from here, and they smile. Retail is one big imagination game. Strangers tell you what they want and expect you to give it to them. Being kind makes that easier.

Once I was working counter, and an angry-looking man came in. He said I have a pretty face. If I ever get in a fight, I should be sure to cover my nose first. Sometimes, these kids come in wearing cargo pants so they can stuff comics down them. Usually I let it happen because whatever, we're corporate. Somewhere I bet there is a huge warehouse with millions of comic books. Nobody's reading those, and hoarding seems worse than stealing books you really do want to read. I mean, if I ever stole anything I'd feel so guilty I'd read it every night.

Rosie's dad wrote a book that was made into a movie. There are alien dragonflies in it, and Rosie's mom is embarrassed because there is lots of sex too. Even more sex than the book. I guess dragonflies have two dicks. They use one to scrape out whatever was there before, and the other to do it themselves. When I imagine this, I don't hear any sound. Rosie's dad gets lots of letters from male scientists and unhappy women.

But the movie made lots of money. Their family got a mini-pool and a dishwasher, and they started taking vacations in planes not cars, so Rosie's mom can't really argue. Now Rosie's dad doesn't take notes at the courthouse anymore. Instead he works on his next book, and he is in the volunteer fire department. There are boots and pants waiting by the office door, ready for him to step into if he gets a call while he's writing. I think it's hard for him to sit still. Once at Parent Teacher Night, Rosie's dad drank five mini-cups of wine and told the science teacher that he liked being a firefighter because it meant he could look into other people's houses. She got a look on her face.

Last summer at the lake, Rosie met a boy who told her about meditation. Not like sitting cross-legged on pillows, but different ways to see shapes and people. One is Looking-Between, so if you are staring at a tree you need to see the shapes around the leaves, as well as the leaves. I tried it and got a headache just like with magic eye paintings. I never see the dinosaur or the ball. I just sit on the couch and wait forever.

Rosie sees them though. Since that night, she started making up her own ways to see. For example, sometimes she will look up images on the computer. Shields, or crests, or illuminated manuscripts. She'll maximize whatever she finds, and then after looking at it awhile, she will lean into the screen and close her eyes. The light on her face looks like she's gazing into a swimming pool.

Rosie says it's a tribute to the religious pilgrims. They travelled days and days on their knees, and when they got to whatever the place, sometimes they would just close their eyes. They would be in The Presence. We do not live in Europe, Rosie says, but because we are modern, we can do it onscreen.

She doesn't like to talk when she is paying tribute. Recently she was looking at a picture of Saint Cecilia, who became a martyr when she lived through three knife-chops to the neck. She died a couple days later, but the whole time she laid there bleeding she was forgiving people and teaching them about Jesus's love. Before she died, she said please turn my home into a church. In Rosie's picture Cecilia is holding a violin, and her skin looks soft. It's scary to see her neck without any chops yet. I don't know about holy bleeding, but I do believe how that story seems real every time I hear it. I don't remember the first time someone told it to me. I wish all churches were houses for people first.

Did you even see any of the ceremony? I asked Rosie, and she said she heard it through a vent in the bathroom wall. That was enough of it for me, she said. Then we walked into the family room to eat buttered tuna and watch a television interview with a lady who almost died. She went over a waterfall in a canoe, flipped at least nine times, and then her legs were pinned underneath the boat. Her lower body turned purple, and her eyes pudged up. She said she felt her spirit separating like two pieces of tape pulling apart. Rosie said yikes, god, and accidentally drooled tuna on the coffee table.

When I can't fall asleep, I imagine books. I rename characters, put chapters in a different order. I kill people to see if it changes anything. After that, if I'm still awake, I imagine John and I are the last people on earth. Everyone else is half-squid half-ghost. When we walk through town, we see tentacles curving around the buildings. The tentacles are pink-orange and gold. They curve like sound and hold the light. I make John and I walk around downtown until it's morning. We walk and walk until I wake.

When we don't have to work, John and I sit at the diner. Rosie is always invited, but she never picks up her phone. The diner is beige and white, with steel-edged tables and chairs that glint in the afternoon. We sit in the window because you can see almost everything inside and three corners of the parking lot, and the reflection from the lights on the pinball machine.

We sit there a long time, so John brings his computer and I bring a book, only I don't always read it. I pretend I'm sitting in the middle of a clock, so time doesn't mean anything to me but I can look at all the hours, one after the other. I look at my book, out the window, at the register, and then in John's sunglasses, and in them I can see whatever movie he's watching. Once we were eating soggy cherry pie, and he was watching a musical. There were women swimming and waving their arms around, and plants. The film was black and white, but you could tell how dark and kiss-proof everyone's lipstick was, even in the water.

The diner staff isn't very big, and I know most everyone else from other places, like when they come into Chapters or I see them at church, or else their clothes look expensive and then I figure they're from the college just outside of town. Anyone in cowboy boots with bows or colored stitching is from the college. But there is one girl. Her nametag says Louise, and I never see her anywhere else. Her hair is black, long and heavy, and she wears silver jewelry. There is a stick and poke cat inside her right elbow, and because it's summer outside and there's no air in the diner, we see it every day. He has six whiskers and one is a little hopscotched, like Louise winced when it hurt extra.

John sighed and tossed his sunglasses on the table. Some cherry filling sprayed on the right lens. I should just give this up huh? he said, jutting out his chin at Louise and at her hair, which is dyed so the sun doesn't catch it. You know? he said, and I said no I didn't. I had no idea what he was talking about. Well, if she was into me she would have said something by now, right? he said. Maybe there's no spark. I said John don't be a moron, you've never even talked to her.

I shouldn't have to talk to her, he said. It should just happen. Otherwise, even if we started dating, I'd always wonder if she was just humoring me. That's stupid, I said, what if she's just shy? How would you know? he said, you've never dated anyone. I mean, I'm no good at it but at least I try. I got quiet and drank coffee and swished it around my teeth.

Okay I said, but John, even I didn't know you liked her. You haven't done anything but come here every day we're off work. Sometimes you don't even talk to me when we're here. He glared, so I stood up to pay for us. John is dumb sometimes. I can't read his mind. But then at the register Louise said hey, I don't usually do this, but you seem smart. You read. Want to do something after work tomorrow?

I had two days off from Chapters and John was being a moron, so I said yes, and I didn't ask if he could come too. Maybe having friends besides John and Rosie would be good. Mr. Green doesn't count. Okay rad, Louise said, and she handed me her phone number. It was written ready-to-go on the wrong side of some receipt paper. She must've been waiting for me. The handwriting was tiny and cartoon-paw-round. I'm done at six, Louise said, so come by then? Okay, I said. See you.

When I sat back down, John said oh that makes sense! She didn't want to date me, she wants to date you. I looked at him. What the hell? I said. John, she probably just wants to hang out. She said I seemed smart. Right, he said. That's what that means. You just don't know. I got mad and said John, let's go. Everything doesn't have to be about sex.

John and I go to the diner all the time. Sometimes we go so much that I forget we went home in-between. We know when the new pies come and all the songs on the jukebox, and if we're getting real food we sit in June's section. June always says happy birthday, because one day she'll be right and that's a sure bet. Half the time she comps our cheese fries, and she yells at John when all he eats are grape jelly packets. She says don't those taste like Band-Aids? You got the cheese for free, why the heck are you eating Band-Aids?

Usually June's church is having a drive, so I bring her Ziploc bags full of Mom's yogurt lids, rinsed and smoothed. For every three dozen tops, someplace in Africa gets a cow. In exchange, the yogurt company sends these little gold pins with udders attached. June pins them to her name-tag. By now she has four dangling udders plus six customer service stars, so pouring coffee, she sounds like kindergarteners in music class. John laughs when she leans over to grab our cups and plates. She always wink-clucks, says oh shush kids. Once John's mom came in with us and said I hope that woman knows what she's doing. Africa is a big place. It's ignorant thinking otherwise. Ignorant is probably the meanest word John's mom says.

John always has cigarettes on him. He steals them from his mom's cartons, but he never has a whole pack and he never really inhales. Half the time the ends are bent because he keeps them loose in his pocket. When he smiles, John looks like himself as a four-year-old, and then I wonder what his baby would look like, if they would have the same teeth. John's hair smells like no filters and sea spray.

When June came with our milkshakes, John said oh, so our friend here has a date tonight. He didn't say it was Louise. I hit him and he said, what? You do. Honey! Good, said June. Thank God. She put her hand on my shoulder. How are you feeling about it, love? Like throwing up, I said. Oh, you'll be fine pumpkin, she says. Who wouldn't love you? Lots of people, I want to say, but I didn't.

On one whole wall of the diner, safe from the sun, there is a big piece of art made from tin and lights and paint. It is a scene. A lake and fields, and a little church with a graveyard and all these roads. There is a switch on the side, and when it's flipped the ducks go around on a wheel and fireworks go off in regular patterns. When I was little, I thought it was a story. Now it's just a map. It's been in the corner so long I forget it's there.

Next day John was at Starlite and I still had an hour before Louise got off, so I tried not to throw up and I walked by the Exotic Pet Store. If you stand by the fish tanks you can see when the bus comes. After that the diner's not too long a ride. I don't know anyone who actually has an exotic pet, but the store stays in business. They sell seahorses and lean-looking sad-eyed cats, and witchy lizards and snake cages. I always look at the cat-toy aisle because those shapes are blobs, like staring into light then closing your eyes and pressing down on the lids. John swears his neighbor has a snake, a snake in a foggy tropical case smack dab in the living room, but I've never seen it. Whenever we walk by the curtains are drawn. If I had a snake I'd be scared he would get out and then be mad at me for keeping him in a cage.

While I waited I thought about Louise, Louise and her black and white striped shirt like she's late for a boat. I don't know how to kiss anyone who isn't family. I guess you just start. Someday I'll say hey, I live with my parents and have a year of high school left, but by then we'll have our own routines so it won't matter.

Then the bus came and we drove past the teacup store, the turnoff for the college. The Catholic bookstore, the place that makes Irish lace, and the place that sells all different kinds of jerky. Then we drove the boulevards. One house had a bunch of kids out between the carport and the front door, modeling new summer clothes for their mom and her camera. The littlest brothers had the same stripes on their pants. It must've been a sale.

Maybe I've never gone out with anyone before because I was saving up. Because this will be perfect, and secretly I'm a natural. Also maybe I was wrong, only ever thinking about dating guys. When the grocery store came up, I got off the bus and bought a box of strawberry coconut ice cream bars for Louise. We could eat them and talk about them. That's ten minutes right there at least.

When I finally got to the diner, June was working the counter, and Louise wasn't anywhere. I almost threw up for real. That darkwater feeling like my body doesn't want to be where it is. It's rejecting something.

In my pocket was the receipt with Louise's number. Her voicemail sounded like violins in a tin can. I felt dumb and young, and not good with time and my voice is stupid and I hung up. Whatever. Maybe John wanted to microwave burritos after work. Watch something subtitled on the computer.

But she called right back. You came! I thought maybe you didn't come. Oh no, I said, all friendly, like how could I not come? I was just buying you ice cream. Okay cool, she said. Come around back, I'm smoking. When I saw Louise I realized I was wearing the same shirt as yesterday. I hope she knows I shower. To breathe, I focused on the hard flat bone in the middle of my chest. Concentrate on that. Imagine it's one curved, smooth bone like half an Easter egg. That would be easier. Hey, said Louise, grinding out a cigarette with the heel of her jelly sandal. Let's walk around the lake she said, and I said okay, cool.

The lake is a fast heavy blue, full of mean geese and college kids, and babies in ruffle-butt swimsuits. Sometimes I worry about the babies and the geese. It's the only water in town, so everybody takes their boats here, which are usually old and staggery, with motors that sound like drunk beehives. But it's very small, so three days a week people go around the lake clockwise, and the other days, to switch it up and also to protect aquatic life, they go around the other way. Once John and I were sunbathing with Rosie when they blew the whistle to switch. It felt special. Some of the boats turn so quickly that the water whitens to froth. When it does that I think about rabies, or the wind.

Louise and I unwrapped an ice cream sandwich each, and we ate them while we walked. Near the dock there's a big wall of gun-color plaques with names on them. They say For Dad or I Love You, or RIP. One said Zippy's, who must have been a dog, and another THE OPERA. The wall went up when I was eight. People had to pay for the plaques, and they couldn't be dirty words. The trophy shop etched in the names. It took a long time to fill the whole thing.

Louise and I made up stories about people who bought each other plaques. People were in love or guilty afterwards, or else just advertising. Louise finger-combs back her hair a bunch. She keeps things in her hands, cigarettes or popsicle sticks or whistling grass. Her hands are big, and elegant as fans.

I'm in a band, she said. We're New Minotaur. I play drums. Right, so she must be one of the punk kids. I looked at her arms, which were like pipe cleaners wrapped with pipe cleaners. For our album cover, said Louise, I covered my chest in craft fur and took a photo on the street in the dark. It wasn't dumb. Sometimes when people do that it's dumb, but this wasn't. Cool, I said, and I meant it. I liked her.

Louise and I walked by some apartments near the library, and I thought how nice it would be, living there with her. Reading. Watching people reading. If you could live in a library. We could have candles and rugs and be warm. Louise looked like she got cold a lot. Let's go to my place, she said. I can drive. There was coconut on her cheek. Instead of telling her or brushing it off, I just stared and thought about skin.

So what do you do? Louise asked. Her dashboard was covered with straw wrappers and chemical sugar packets. A bobble dog. I write I guess, I said. I dunno. I go to shows. We were at a stoplight and Louise looked at me around her glasses, which were open-mouth-big and dark, plastic painted gold. Wait, she said. Wait. How old are you? Oh god. I'm old,

I said. I've been around. I figured she was, like, twenty-four or something. Didn't want her to think I was a baby. She shrugged, nodded. Made a left turn. Didn't tell me her age either, but whatever. It doesn't matter.

Where Louise lived had folding chairs on the porch, and orange plastic flowers in buckets, and curtains made from Saturday morning cartoon sheets. It smelled like the inside of a season-old beach bag, but then we walked down the hallway and it smelled more like bread. It was kind of dinnertime. I wanted to sit on the kitchen counter and wait to see who else came into the room.

Want a beer? Louise asked. Okay, I said. I guess so. I'd never had one, but whatever. Secretly I'm a natural. Waiting for Louise to say something else, I leaned against the refrigerator door. It was jammed with magnets, as decoration, not to hold things. Birds, red shoes, skylines. A tree. Here, she said, scratching her ankle with her toe. They're by the juice. Let me show you.

Louise came towards me, her arm the color of oysters and throats and milk, her bones snap-thin. That winky cat tattoo. I didn't move, and I ignored feeling wanting to turn into purple smoke. I looked Louise dead on and her lips, and I parted mine and I came towards her, too. Oh, she said.

Oh! She went backwards and swallowed a laugh. Oh honey, that's—that's not what I meant. Ugh. Now I wanted to be liquid. Pour myself down the hallway. Suddenly her face became different. Not mean though, just thinking.

You know, actually. I didn't eat so it would be dumb to drink,
Louise said. Do you want cereal instead? We have cereal and
string cheese. No, I said, hearing blood in my ears and trying
not to faint. My smooth plastic egg chest. I guess it's late. I
should probably just go home. Alright, said Louise. I'll drive
you, but I'll hop in the bathroom first. While she did, I peeled
one of the magnets off the fridge—a fish on a checkerboard
background—and put it in my pocket. I didn't feel guilty about
it either. It didn't feel like stealing, just like writing it down.
Writing down moves so I don't forget them later. I'll have to
tell John how we can't go to the diner for a while. He'll be okay.
You can watch movies on a computer anywhere.

In the car Louise turned on the radio. It was that afternoon
show on the college station. Those girls don't always work the
board right, and sometimes they are nervous about liking
what they like, which is dumb. Music can't make you sick. I
remember once I was making a mixtape for John and I sat
four or five minutes, deciding whether to use a song that had
fuck in it. Then I realized how dumb I was being. I didn't ask
the band to use that word.

We listened quietly a while. I wondered if Louise thought,
what kind of a moron tries to kiss people in front of a
refrigerator? If I'd asked first maybe she would've let me. I
looked at her fingernails, which were all different blues and
one gold, snap against the boring-color steering wheel. She
reached over to roll down the passenger window, and her
hair brushed my knee. Breeze poured into the car like water,

like we just went over a bridge and hit water and needed a new plan.

In our quiet I tried to think of something to say that wouldn't be sexual or impersonal. I remembered the last book I read on break at the store. It was about space, so half-magic and half-math, but the one before that was about octopi. Did you know, I asked Louise, that octopi are observational learners? She looked at me with one eyebrow up. No she said, I didn't. They are, I said. After the mothers give birth they stop eating and die, so the little ones have to learn from what they see, not what they're taught. She laughed. So like, one octopus could start windmill swimming, just to be funny, and the little ones would be funny too? I guess, I said, only octopi aren't really creative.

You're a secret weirdo, huh? Louise asked, and I felt proud, not embarrassed. Tell me what else you know about octopuses she said, and switched off the radio. I didn't panic. Well I said, last week John was late picking me up from work, and I was so tired I thought I might fall asleep at the bus stop. So while I waited for him I read about octopi. Cool, she said, like of course you did. They have three hearts I told her, and their brains wrap around their throats. That's rad, she said, like you'd tap your neck if you had an idea. Yeah, I said, I guess you would.

What's cool too is how they leave bad situations. They'll run headfirst, which looks like ribbons from behind because they don't have skeletons. They can slide off hooks, because no bones catch. Or they'll shoot a wall of ink, as disguise or distraction. The ink has a special chemical that makes creatures want to fall in love. Suddenly I saw John's face, like what the hell are you doing, going on about octopi? Are you four? When they are scared, all of a sudden, I told Louise, octopi turn pale and flatten out like capes.

Also, I said, in Hawaiian myth octopi are the lone survivors of an alien dynasty universe. And their biggest parts are their arms, so in a way they see by touch. Through texture, which is different than feeling along the walls in a dark room so you don't bump the table. Yeah said Louise, it totally is. When her arms move, you can see the cords. Love at first sight is maybe seeing how someone's muscles work. Then we saw my house. The lights were off, but Mr. Green was probably home next door.

I'm sorry I tried to kiss you, Louise, I said. I didn't mean it to be weird. It's okay, she said. Dude, I really just wanted to hang out with you. Yeah, well now I know, I said. I wished I didn't have a body, that I could close my eyes and waft. I unbuckled my seatbelt and cannonballed into the house. I didn't look, but I heard her tires moving away. It was nice of her to wait until I was inside.

Rosie used to go out with John and I a lot, before and after they dated, but not since the abortion. Her parents don't know about it. The death, or the relationship. They don't even know she ever had sex. One of the college boys who wears flip flops year-round saw us three leaving the clinic. Now everyone thinks Rosie's lost or a witch. They hover and mack, and now at parties, instead of trying to sleep with her, they invite her to support groups.

At school, the Gay Straight Alliance handed out cards saying it was okay for boys to want to sleep with boys, but not to actually do it. That feeling must stay burrowed deep in your heart. What the hell. It's already so hard, figuring out what you want, and once you do, then you have to lie to yourself your whole life? That has to be wrong. It does not seem any more complicated than that to me.

So I made a fist with the card in it, then went and sat in a corner of the bat cage to breathe. The bat cage is the only place where teachers don't bother you and students don't assume you're making out. But Kate, the art teacher who eats potato chips in the hallway on break, she saw me and came in and said, right on. Nobody's perfect. The Bible got many things right, but maybe it messed this one up. You know, sometimes a part is bad but that doesn't mean all of it is.

Suddenly Kate looked tender in her paisley dress and round brown glasses. Those boxing gloves hanging on the wall behind her like alien cauliflowers. Kate has a husband, a librarian, and he loves her very much. Last year I guess they chaperoned prom together. It seems easy for them.

Hmm, I said. I guess so, I said. I wanted to say, but lots of different people wrote the Bible and maybe some of them never went outside. Do you know how it feels to never ask permission? To never wear a costume? But the bell rang so instead I said I have to go to math now. Kate said okay, honey.

After Louise left I didn't feel like staying inside, so I sat on our porch until the lights went on at Mr. Green's. Then I went over there.

At home Mr. Green always wears this old navy blue coat. I think it's silk. He bought it with a buddy after a three-martini-lunch in New York for too much money, but if he wears it every day eventually it will pay for itself. Sometimes he sleeps in it. The coat sleeves start right where his shoulders end and hit his wrists just past a watch, which is how Mom says you know a good fit.

Mr. Green keeps a liquor shaker in the freezer, and a postcard of four buffalo jumping off a cliff, and in the backyard, those bluebird feeders. I always tell John he could come over too, but John says no way. That guy creeps me out. The one time we did go over together, John saw the upstairs room, which is all mirrors. There's no wallpaper, just mirrors and plants. It's beautiful. Each wall reflects or is only leaves. John felt weird because he couldn't think of any one thing everyone could do in there, but I like rooms having options. For example, it would be a good place to dance.

The front door was unlocked like always. Heya kid, said Mr. Green, drinking water from a yellow glass. Last week he said a lady made it for him. Old girlfriend. I guess she was great. She was a redhead and a little butterfingered, so there were glass-blowing burns all over her arms. They blistered into pink and stayed forever. It was sexy, said Mr. Green, how into the work she was. It stayed with her. How was your day, kid?

I told him about Louise, and the refrigerator, and he laughed. Shit kid, you're supposed to give it a second! Were you sitting down? Did you make her food?

How was I supposed to make her food? I said. I mean come on, it wasn't my house! Plus I was nervous. Mr. Green looked at me and put his hands on his knees, fingers all spread out. He bark-laughed. Look kid, you gotta make people food. You don't ask, you just walk into their kitchen and do it. A little charm, a little class goes a long way, kid. Know your spices. He stood up, went to the fridge, and came back with a beer. The can had a ship on it. I've never seen that kind in the yards after baseball games. Ships make me think of fathoms, which are only six feet, and being surrounded by ocean, that's like getting a hug from a grown man.

Mr. Green wears a turquoise arrow ring on his pinky. When he opened the beer he used his thumb to dent in a little notch right under where you drink. Makes it go down smoother, kid. Try it. I took a sip and wiped my mouth with the back of my hand. Better kid, right? Smoother that way? I said yes, sure. I've never drank beer before, but I didn't want him to know. It tasted soapy. He drank the rest of the can.

The college's baseball team is pretty good, and sometimes I work at the bookstore during games. Usually those afternoons are slow. Just outside the gate they sell these ruby red balloons. When you're a kid, it's a big deal. Your mom will buy you a balloon, then you carry it in and hold it through the National Anthem and everything, and when we score our first run you let your balloon go. Then the whole town knows. It looks beautiful from a distance, like spiritual death and the stadium is the corpse. The balloons lift and we are all still on the ground.

Sometimes now I am in the Chapters parking lot when the balloons first go. From that distance it's like a big red flock of birds. I think about all the poor real birds, finding the balloons and maybe choking on them. Once I read this book, and this guy talked about how rage is like a blood-filled egg. Now I think about that when I see the balloons let loose. Popped, they'd be gashes. Stars of color everywhere.

After ten-fifteen and sometime before ten-forty-five, the checkout supervisor takes a break with the other guy from children's. The checkout supervisor has almost no hair at all. He looks like a vampire on purpose, and plays Moog in a two-person band with his wife. The other guy wears leopard-print boots every day, and purple pants. He's so skinny I could circle his wrist with my thumb and pinkie finger.

He is in a secret society of knights. He met them on the Internet. For initiation they flew him out to Vegas, where they met him at the airport and then left him in a dark cave for hours, blindfolded with a couple granola bars in his lap. It is an exercise in trust, he explained to me, because you know they'll come back. You just don't know when. When they took the blindfold off, he was officially in the order. I tried to think of something I want so badly that I'd sit in the dark forever, and I couldn't. Everything I want is people.

John's mom's hair is bright red, so when she stands in the right place in the kitchen it makes a halo. She's always chewing licorice, or a pen or a hangnail, and since she quit smoking she keeps candies in her pocket. The gleaming kind, grandma candies in primary colors like butterscotch and cinnamon. She can unwrap them with one hand and two twists.

John's mom cuts hair, so if I'm over when she comes home and people weren't crabby that day, she'll give me a trim at the table. I like her wrist on my neck, and sometimes my back shivers when she does around my ears. Her lotion smells like orange vanilla milk powder, and there's glitter in it.

She works at the only fancy salon, the one with a little fountain in front and your choice of tea or coffee while you wait. There is a pretzel stand next door so sometimes it smells like roses and ylang ylang, sometimes hot cheese. The women at the salon look complicated and don't talk a lot. Their lips are tight, quick puckers with matte lipstick. John calls it anus mouth. His mom says when you wash their hair you feel the raised line behind their ears. That's how you know they had work done.

If John's mom is really tired when she gets home, but on her feet too long to sleep, she just sits at the table looking like someone else. Usually John puts out a box of crackers. He says do you want wine, or will you read us tarot? Last time she read mine I got the tower card. At first I was scared because it's all tumble and lightning, all falling screaming people and stars. John's mom saw my face and said don't worry, sweetheart.

They weren't supposed to be up in that tower anyway. Now they get to start over fresh.

For a while John's mom was on this kick about good practice experiences for being an adult. She made him learn to iron and to bake apple pie, which is funny because she never bakes anything but slice-and-warm freezer cookies. She buys them in bulk after holidays, because they never go bad and every color is pretty. Last year for the Fourth we ate Valentine's hearts.

John did his best but the pie came out black, and nobody wanted to throw it all away so we ate the filling over ice cream. It tasted like cinnamon and grit. It wasn't fruit-colored, but it wasn't terrible either.

After that, John's mom started thinking about what John's dad would've taught him if he cared about anyone besides himself, and one thing was how to buy appliances. John's mom never bought appliances before either, so she told us to go on our own and try our best. It's practice, she said. You're not really going to buy an oven tonight.

When we got to the store we went up to the third floor, which is where they keep the washing machines and dryers for sale. John started to be like are they going to think we're weird? I said no, it's normal. How else do people buy washing machines? Then he said but maybe we aren't those people, so he made up a story about how we were. We were in love and moving into our first new place together. I said yes, we are.

The saleslady was nice. Her fingernails had tiny ladybugs on them and her name tag said Marie. Marie knew lots about washing machines, including which got the best value out of what soap. She asked us what part of town we lived in, and I couldn't tell if she was sincere or just playing along. John said up by the lake, and that we would have BBQs on our porch, soon as we got it all set up. The lady said that sounded wonderful and she was right. It did. After awhile, we said thank you. We will be in touch after some comparison shopping.

The whole thing went pretty quickly so we had time for hot dogs. I didn't like how my brain felt and wanted that to stop, so I said John, do you ever think maybe we spend so much time together because we really are in love? He started laughing. Mustard came out the corner of his mouth, and I hit him in the elbow. That's mean, I said. It took me a long time to say that.

When Grandpa married Grandma, he gave her a clock and said here. This is solid. We will have a house together, and this clock will be on the wall and in the middle of the night you'll wake and hear it, and I'll be here too. I bet she rolled her eyes at him, but secretly also I bet she liked it. The promise, the clock. That he even said it.

Dad liked that story too, so now we have four clocks including that first one. They all go off every fifteen minutes, all four chimes together like a fishtail braid. Grandma's is wood and pearl, and a little moon goes around with the hours.

When someone who's not John is over, they look at me like wow, you guys have the craziest doorbell.

My grandparents died before I started kindergarten, and before that they were in the hospital a lot, but there are photos of them smiling. She had a tiny waist, and he put his hands on it. He wore bright white shirts all the time. They were smokers and bowlers, and every Friday they went out dancing and to eat, no matter how little the kids were. They really liked each other honey, said Mom. Like not everybody does. Whenever they went out anywhere, Grandma took a coffeecup in her purse for the extra butter, to cook with later. Sometimes she'd pop in the rolls too, for making toast before going to sleep.

Her chocolate cake had coffee grounds and sour cream in it, and brown sugar frosting. She froze the extra in cubes and ate it like candy, cold from the fridge after the last baby went to bed. Mom says sometimes she couldn't sleep, so she'd go out to the kitchen and see Grandma there in her bouquet of flowers housedress, leaning against the fridge and chewing. One arm folded around her waist like a belt.

After I decided to dye my hair, John and I stood in front of the counter almost ten minutes. I wanted green, but the one they had looked like sour pop and it actually really frightened me, thinking about lying in bed at night and that was the color of my hair. It would never turn off. Like when I was little at Christmas, and we'd go by the department store display. Back at home I always wanted to cry, thinking about those ice skaters spinning around on that lit-up foil pond. Back and forth all night long. Cold figure eight forever.

John could tell I was freaking out, so you should do purple, he said. Purple's you, he said, plus it's a dark color so we won't need as much bleach. Okay, I said. Sure, great. I like it when John decides.

His mom was working late so we had the whole house to ourselves, his whole quilted-together house with the jewel-colored chairs and chipped pretty dishes. They moved when we were in sixth grade, after the divorce, and when I first came over, John said welcome. Quick, sit in all the places so you feel comfortable everywhere. I made him do it too.

Their fridge is sensible and easy, everything goes straight into the microwave or comes out of the package. Our kitchen is always four steps and at least half an hour away from dinner. Measuring out flour while making the pie, we found a lacquer box with a peony on top and pictures inside. Foggy photobooth photos of breasts and a necklace, and somebody's finger with nail polish on it. John said it wasn't his mom's hand, he didn't know whose hand it was, stop. John misses his dad.

When he went in the bathroom for a minute, I smelled the inside of the box. It was kind of lemony. When you take those kind of photos, I wonder if your lover is supposed to be with you in the booth, or if you take it on your own to send later, in a letter or under a door. I guess it could happen both ways.

We sat in the kitchen because it had tile and John's mom said she'd kill us if we dyed the carpet. It's funny, hair is the one thing she really could teach us how to do, but when we asked she said no sweethearts, I just cut it. So I sat on the spinny chair, and we got out a garbage bag and cut a hole in it and put my head through. We got the cranky little radio from the shower and set it to the college station again. It was a new album by an old band, but the songs sounded so different. I love that. That means something happened in-between, in their actual lives, even if the lyrics don't say so.

While John painted on the dye, I played with the little box of crayons his mom keeps by the phone. One is called Magic Mint, which John says should be an STD. I held the crayons in my lap, because if you look down your eyes burn less. I said Violet Blue would be a good pen name. John said that's great, your name'd match your hair, and I said not for me, just in general. He said oh.

After an hour and ten minutes, then ten more to be safe, we walked into the bathroom. The water down the drain looked like a puppet melted. I looked in the mirror and it was perfect, like violet violets or someone rubbed candy in my hair. I said John it's perfect and he said duh, I knew it would be.

When I got home Dad was waiting up, asleep in the chair. He was snoring in gray basketball shorts and a Miraculous Medal, mouth open. I went to get milk, and the refrigerator door woke him up. He said hi sweetheart, saw my hair and said oh, he didn't think I was going to do the whole thing. Why did I do the whole thing?

Because I like purple, I said. Plus we had a whole box, and the dye doesn't keep. John helped. Well, Dad said, okay. Just as long as you're not sad. You're not sad, are you honey? No, I said. No I'm not sad.

My boss at the bookstore is Steve. He is good at routines. Steve's coat is always buttoned clean and there are long neat lines of safety pins on his backpack. He's pretty flexible otherwise though, like he doesn't care if I read from the music encyclopedia when there's no line at the registers. My favorite so far are oboes. You have to really wet the reed and warm them up before they sound right.

When I started working here I was a freshman, and now I'm basically a senior and in that time Steve quit drinking. Now he lives with his mom, soberly, and he shows up on time in the mornings. Only it doesn't make Steve look happy. He looks like he's out of air. When I ask, he says I don't understand. He did something he can never ever fix. The guilt of it. Steve is ready to go on dates again, but it's hard. He lost his license after a DUI. Nobody wants to go by your mom's house on a first date when you're almost forty, he says. I keep saying you're thinking too much Steve, just try and it'll be fine. He winces like I'm just too young.

We have a funny relationship. Steve's twenty years older than I am, but we both live at home so there is a lot in common. Sometimes when I cash out, he slips in front of me to check the drawer. His shirt smells like dryer sheets and I can see his shoulder blades. Ever since Steve quit drinking, it's like he got sharper. I keep thinking maybe I should call after hours, in case he's sad.

Our store's a chain so there are set storytime themes, all for new books they want people to buy. Each week comes with a costume. It's Steve's job to wear it, and mine to zip him in. Corporate mails us four at a time, and those boxes are neat to open because everything's all scrambled. Crowns and hats, ears and ribbons. You figure it out because there's a picture printout of how the outfit's supposed to look.

This week was a strong orphan. I didn't know the book, but she had red braids and a big foam head with freckles, and soft black shoes and I guess she looked like she could handle bad guys. Once you zip up her back, nobody knows anything about your own body. Once Steve was inside, the orphan's face became scary. Those open eyes, a mouth that can't react. Body in a body. I bet that head gives him a headache even more than the snowman did. Anyway, next I took Steve's elbow and we walked out together. He can't see a thing inside her head, so I always help him not bump into display tables.

The babies were already there. They are maybe four-years-old, just before kindergarten. Dressed in superhero T-shirts, clutching chewed-looking toys in thawing pastels. They act just like drunk college kids at shows, so I feel comfortable around them but not their mothers, who sip fancy coffees and wear sweatshirts that drape. They have chunky peanut butter diamonds on their bird-bone fingers. They chit chat. It's a thing, the chummy morning mommies.

Steve always asks if there's one without a ring, because he can't really see when he's in the costume. I always say I look, but actually I don't. Those women eat power greens salad. They dip their forks into the dressing and are not flexible about cheese. They would vaporize Steve and his lines of safety pins.

After he's settled on the chair, I stand up and press play. Of course you can't talk when you're zipped into the costume, so Steve just holds up the pictures and the CD reads everything to the kids. It does all the voices. I guess everyone likes it okay. Steve says once he fell asleep inside the snowman but nobody knew. Once I was really tired too, so I sat down on a folding chair, and a little boy just came over and sat in my lap. He smelled like sweat and raspberry blue flavor. There was a black rubber stain on his knee. His mom must've taken him to the playground that morning.

After work we went to the quick mart parking lot. It's right across the street from the Chinese food place, so you can get takeout egg rolls and cherry freezes at once, eat them both in the car. John likes pairing foods one juicy, one sweet. He doesn't like sugar if there's no texture.

Know what would be great? John said. His lips were burned poppy red from the sauce. It looked like he'd bitten them. What? I said, stuffing hot cabbage in my mouth. A polar bear juggling fire, said John. It was weird, but that's a beautiful idea I said, unwrapping the chocolate bar we got to split. A polar bear juggling fire. It's perfect. You should be that for Halloween.

Nobody else talks about polar bears with me. Everything else matters either not at all or way too much. Sometimes the whole rest of my life feels like dumbly polite conversations at the bookstore, at school, home. It makes me feel like a sheep pelt. It makes me like church because you don't have to make anything up there. But still when I got that pamphlet from the Alliance, the one that said boys shouldn't sleep with boys, it felt wrong like a stop sign. So wrong that I felt wrong, and so I wondered if I was gay. If I am queer in solidarity. I told Rosie and she said oh my god, no. Stop.

I never learned to drive. But there was no reason to because I always took the bus or a bike, or I rode with John, which is nicer anyway. I like being able to read. But now that I'm eighteen, Mom is trying to teach me how. Saturday afternoons in the church parking lot is the plan. The lot is big and holy and blacktop and this helps her, I think. She can't see anything bad happening there. Of course we never go that fast.

We never go half that fast. We go just before five o'clock Mass and make fifteen minutes of left turns, fifteen of right. We are so far from the freeway. We make these big loose loops while Mom grips her knitting. She presses down on an invisible gas pedal which makes me feel like I'm drowning, so I try to think about other things instead. Things like choruses or imaginary ships, or Alex Hardman's shoulders, which are round and firm like squeeze cheese in a tube. I say the alphabet backwards, think about what if my lungs changed colors. At one end of the parking lot, some parents painted a big happy crayon map of the United States. Florida looks like a leg, so I try amputating it with my wheels each time. I imagine it sliding off the country like a feather.

Two out of four Saturdays there's Bible School too, so we have to look out for kids. I know all their coat colors. One of the girls, Mollie, wears a raincoat with umbrellas printed on it. She lives down the street, and sometimes I see her waiting with her mom for the bus. Mollie is nearly deaf, so everyone else always works really hard to make her feel normal. Sometimes this backfires because well, she isn't normal. She can't hear.

But her friends are cool. They all just learned sign language. They all sit together on the tire swing, hands like ducks flying until somebody makes a joke and suddenly everyone laughs. Mollie's laughter takes over, like when you are angry and stand up quickly. It's loud too, snorts and hey hey hey. It makes me think she'll be a good dancer when she's older, if she can feel the beat through the floor. Or maybe they can turn the bass up high and let her hold a balloon.

Well you'll have clover turns down, said John, one day in his dad's really old car, rolling a pencil over, across, through his fingers while we sat in the parking lot after his shift. There is always fifteen minutes between John wiping ice cream glaze off the counters and his boss turning off the lights. That's when I come by. We wait in the car so she can't make him do busy work with pizza toppings, or listen to her talk about her sex life.

Your mom can't just let you leave the parking lot, huh? said John. Nope, I said. My uncle taught me on the freeway when I was twelve, John said. He'd just bring a bunch of beer for himself and grab the wheel if I got too close to the median. That must've been nice, I said. It was, said John.

It was raining in the parking lot and lights shone like Christmas in the windshield. John's boss was taking forever. We guessed one of the kids peed in the back or something. It was almost dinner, so I got out the bag of doughnuts John's mom keeps hidden under the seat. We didn't talk, we just turned up the radio and sat licking sugar from our fingers until his boss walked out and waved. Yelled okay, you can go home now guys. We're good. I like being called guys.

John is allergic to peanuts, so on days when he has long shifts and I don't have to go in, I buy a pack of peanut butter cups for breakfast and eat them in the parking lot in the sun. The time alone is important. I don't talk to anyone and I don't feel like I have to either. I guess I think about food a lot, but when you eat, that's how you know the day is moving along.

John says his throat closes up right away, even from a crumb. Even from smelling it. Like, the aura of the peanut. Sometimes I get scared there'll be a piece in my hair and it will get in his mouth, and I'll kill him before we get home. I imagine his mom's face and immediately feel bad, like imagining it makes it closer to reality. If I killed John, I would have to name a baby after him.

Suddenly that night at dinner, hamburger and peas with noodles in mushroom cream and breadcrumbs, Dad was seeing what time the game started and I said, Mom? Mom this is stupid. I'm sorry but the world's not a parking lot, and I need to learn how to drive. One mean burst from nowhere. It surprised us both, I think.

I love you I said, but Mom, we never leave the parking lot. She blinked and swallowed, frowned at her fork, but the next day she made me an appointment at the driving school. Just left a note about it on the fridge. Love you, sweetie!

Robert is my instructor. His car is small and tan. He smells like it, like MSG and nicotine and other small, tan things. Robert's eyes are maybe a little mean, or maybe he's always looking into too much light. His hands are gentle, notebook-paper-colored, and his hair falls into his face. I could imagine him eating a TV dinner on a couch, or cat-sitting someone's cat. Waiting in line for limited tickets.

The first time I got in the car Robert said hey, kid. Hey, I think maybe I forgot to take something this morning, so be nice, okay? Okay, I said. Man I just want to learn to drive. Mom paid for three sessions in three weeks.

We always went to the drug store first, where Robert bought three mini candy bars and two of those fudge squares wrapped in cloudy paper, the kind stickered gold. The clerk was named Jamie. Guys named Jamie, said Robert, get a lot of sex. We split the fudge and then Robert told me to get behind the wheel.

It made me nervous, how he said sex, but not bad nervous. Just like when I looked in my aunt's medicine cabinet at Thanksgiving and saw the box of tampons. Like oh right, there's your body.

Is he a freak? asked John. Because he sounds like a freak. The car smelled like onion rings and John's right eyebrow was smudgy because he was putting on eyeliner when we hit a speed bump. He doesn't always wear eyeliner, just sometimes. To see how it works. You guys should sleep together or something, John said.

Barf no, I said. He has a girlfriend. Plus man, Robert's serious. He wants to be a screenwriter. When he's not driving he writes scripts, and sometimes he talks to me about them. I tell him what's missing. Where there could be more feeling.

There's a really good one about Native American princesses who are also secret agents, I said. He said I could be in it if it sells. Uh-huh, said John. With your hair. Hey also, you're not Indian so that would be appropriation. Well sure, I said. But it's a good script so far. Uh huh, said John, making his mouth a line so he could do the other eye.

Before I was born, there was a baby food plant where everyone worked, but now there's just the college. It's pretty big, and nobody there talks to us like we matter. I get angry with them and their money. Their pretty coats. How when national television comes to film sports, they change the flags to the school's colors, not ours. Every other time of year, they're ours. How on game day, the muffin frosting is orange and blue. The windsocks at the store are orange and blue. Even the mortician has an orange and blue casket option.

That's all terrible, but still you only get one home. At work I read this article that said the last thing you remember on your deathbed is the map of where you were born. I don't want to remember home with sports flags spearing it like toothpicks through an olive. Maybe I should learn the names of trees. John said I should stop harping. Sports is spectacle, and people like it because there is a chance someone'll do something nobody else has ever done before. I said fine, well then you clean up the yards after those games.

On Parent Weekend, everyone's dad brings cheap beer to play flip cup. They leave those red cups in our yards, like there's this magical time when you get to be a mess before you get a job. It makes me feel bad when we drive to church on Sundays and all the yards are confettied towards the street. Sometimes Mr. Green is out there with a trash bag and binoculars.

But those students are rich so they do have good shows in their basements, in their rental houses with muddy stairs and couches that smell like beer and hair. They are the right beautiful to bring bands through, and the school gives them money to do it. The trick when you go, besides listening up front unless there's a fight, is putting your backpack in the dryer. That way, when you go up to dance you won't hit people in the teeth. Plus when your keys are in the dryer you never lose them.

Today John had an extra long lunch break, so he drove over to visit me on mine. I could see the pressed-in red bands where the costume was too tight on his wrists. His hair was pressed-down and sweaty. John had three cigarettes and a bottle of that special lotion he bought online. The kind to get rid of smoke smell. I think usually people use it for other things, but it works for smoke smell too. I never smoke a whole cigarette but John doesn't care.

I brought out the bookstore rule book and read him parts while we smoked. Parts like you may not sell cosmetics, cookies, or mints on the job. Before you report a lost child, you must first obtain a complete description, including shoes. No cussing on the floor.

After awhile John looked at the time, panicked, and threw the cigarette into the dumpster without grinding it out first. You doof I said, and then we both jumped in to fish it out. My jeans smelled like cream cheese the whole rest of the day. Before that I never really thought about how cream cheese smelled.

On my breaks, I like shopping in the bookstore. Nobody says can I help you find something, because they know I know anyway. It is pretty much the only place in my life where everyone leaves me alone. Steve says it's criminal to give them money on top of my time. But I figure counting the afternoons I read instead of stock, or stamp my wrists blue with the one-hour parking stamp, I come out ahead.

Sometimes on my way to the bathroom, I see the milk-colored lady in the bodice-ripper section. She wears black and lace and thick glasses. She plops down on the carpet and trails one finger along the seashell-pink and gold and cream covers. Then she picks one, slides it out and licks her lips, reads the jacket copy to herself. Sometimes she puts one hand on her chest and rubs it and sighs. That lady never buys anything, but whatever, she's not bothering anyone. I always want to ask her name, but I don't. Sometimes she smiles at me and I worry I scowl back on accident.

Last night Rosie called for the first time in weeks, said come to a show with me. So we did. All the college kids there came from the baseball game. When games happen it is like nothing else is going on, not even a war. One boy still had popcorn in a paper cone. Caramel and cheese together. One girl had a big green drink with a caterpillar straw. Everyone's face was greasy from the diamond lights. Everyone smelled like that pink powdered soap in the bathrooms, the kind you rub with water to activate. The half-time show, somebody said, was this kid in a big blow-up bowling ball. He won the raffle at the bank, so they strapped him in and rolled him down the field. If he knocked down enough pins, Section Sixteen got free slushies. They were actually kind of gross, said one girl. They were watered down by the time they got to our row.

Oh that's cute, you're in high school! said a girl in lace boots. What are you doing afterwards? I hate when people ask that because really, who knows for sure? Plus that question isn't about you. It's about them expecting you're not going to college. I told her I was going to write, which is half-true, half-because people can't really ask more questions after that. It's not like you're just going to hand them your novel. She said oh that's so sweet! I want to do the same thing. To write for fun, before going to law school probably. Before I have responsibility. But it's not for fun, I almost said. Why would I write just for fun? How does someone not have responsibility? Even if I was rich I'd have responsibility.

Then the drummer came downstairs. He sat at the kit in the corner of the room where the couch usually is, next to the dumpster lamp and a mushy-looking fish tank and one sneaker. This guy had a huge piece of cherry cheesecake on a plate. He just sat down to eat and to watch. He scared me so I turned to Rosie, who was easy to find because her dress had a spiderweb print. She was drinking pink wine from the fridge. We have a secret sign, like a flag. If you run your finger down your eyebrow, then it's time to go. Rosie and I made eye contact, and then I felt okay again.

Eventually, the band started. This kid in the front row kept yelling freebird, and I wanted to elbow his back ribs because I couldn't hear over it. A guy across the room had a skyline tattoo on his arm, but it was too dark to see which city. The girl behind me was kind of cheering, kind of yelping, and I remembered her from the grocery store. She turned all the pineapple upside-down cake boxes upside down, as a thing. The band played a song about our lake. A kid drowned there last summer. Some people think he was drunk, and some people think he was sad.

Then the music zoomed, airplanes taking off, and I thought about the time John and I went to a show here, and his dad's really old car broke down so we slept upstairs. We had a room with a mattress with blue dots. I think they were candy stains, or maybe mirror cleaner.

A couple other people were sleeping on the floor, and after they stopped rustling, John put his arms around me. He never did that before. Usually, when we fall asleep together it's because we can't stay awake. Sleeping like that, you don't have a body, just breath. It is never not brave, falling asleep next to someone in a house without your bedroom in it. Still this felt so different that I started to wonder if maybe I messed up. Maybe we are in love, and I just don't know how it works or feels. That was the first time I thought that way about John. What if nobody ever understands me like he does? What if I'm weird in a bad way?

Maybe I should try to sleep with him. As the music bloomed smaller I thought about John, standing in the Starlite alley on break with the rabbit head under his arm, trying not to ash into the fur. In my head he was lonely. I got some more pink wine from the fridge, and decided to call him and ask him to unlock his front door, and stay up and wait for me to come. I'd tell him I loved him again. I figure when you don't know what to do, you might as well put yourself in the middle of it.

Outside was gritty summer wind. I leaned against the band's van and got out my phone. The crickets sounded big which made me think I was drunk, but then I decided I wasn't because if I was, I wouldn't wonder. John's phone rang and rang and I called it again. Twelve rings. I looked at my old shoes, toes redder with dust. I called one more time, then put my phone in my back pocket. That way, if he called I'd feel it buzz.

Inside again, the band was breaking down and I went back to the fridge. The drummer, cheesecake guy, he came over. He put his hand on my elbow, said hi soft. I noticed how nice his eyebrows were. They kind of floated in front of his face, like right at first when you put on 3D glasses and open your eyes towards the screen. I hadn't noticed them out in the crowd.

He had whiskey and said I was pretty, and he didn't ask me anything about myself. Instead he talked about his new album. It's solo. The songs are ones everyone knows, but the sound is just him. Sometimes people have to be tricked into hearing something new, you know? He winked. If I put out an album of my own songs first, it'd take much longer for people to care.

He had three crosses around his neck. One for Jesus and one for God and one for the Ghost. He had a nice voice and I trusted him. It felt like my face was covered in perfume, or a scarf. If he was in a car, I would sit next to him. Instead I followed him to the porch, where it was just us.

Rosie found me. Her lipstick was run, its color slipped left like she'd wiped her mouth hard with her hand. I'm done here, she said. I'm going home. You okay? Call me in the morning? She waited a beat, like I could go with her if I wanted to. I shook my head. Okay, I said. Okay. I'm okay. I love you. She blinked, and looked at the drummer and then at me. I shook my head, said I'd call her in the morning and I mean it. Rosie! Go.

I put my head in the drummer's neck and said I was moving to New York. It was a new thought, but saying it felt so easy I believed myself too. I was going to eat black and white cookies, and write magazine articles, and cry at the opera. Why not. He said when? Soon, I said. He said well, if you know what's right, what's in your heart, then Jesus will help you. He will walk you towards truth. I looked at the drummer's eyelashes. He put my cup on the stair and took my hand, and we went upstairs.

We laid down on that same mattress. Downstairs the headliner was starting, and through the air vents I could hear pineapple upside-down cake girl sort of shrieking. The drummer took off everything but his crosses. He licked my neck and pulled my hair. He smelled like gas station nachos. There was a black velvet poster on the wall, half a snake of incense in the corner. I watched it go in and out of view behind his shoulder. I figured I was getting this out of the way. The first time always feels like outer space.

Afterwards, we laid shoulders touching, looking at the wet bumps in the ceiling. Thanks for what you said about Jesus, I said, and ran my finger down his arm. I never thought about it like that before. Sure baby, he said. Sure. Hey I'll be right back.

I must've fallen asleep because then it was morning, though no birds yet, and I was still on the mattress. I was cold. I checked for bleeding because I heard sometimes you do, but the mattress was still only stained blue. I pulled up my socks, saw John never called, then crept downstairs to get my purse from the dryer and sneak out back. Pineapple girl was on the couch, her knees folded like a newspaper. Little metallic snores.

In the driveway I texted Rosie. Call me when you wake up, I said. It was too early for the bus so I walked towards the grocery store for fruit and a doughnut, to sit in the parking lot until Rosie called. The sky was huge and smooth, soft, and some people already had flags on their porches, or Uncle Sam windsocks. I felt relieved, like maybe I should pray, but I didn't.

All junior year, even when John and I didn't feel like school, we went to first period drama anyway. That way, at least your name is somewhere. Rosie doesn't care about actually graduating, but we do. Otherwise why go even once? The drama teacher smells like gin and hairspray, and she almost always asks if can she sing Danny Boy before class. We wouldn't mind, would we? We always say no, no of course not, and then she pony-tosses her hair behind her shoulders and stands square. She bleats. The pipes, the pipes. At the end her mouth opens wide and her hands go up, and we all see the pink drip shaking at the back of her mouth. It is very important to open your mouth three fingers high at least.

John and I always sat in the back and winced, and wondered how drunk she was. Sometimes we played fortunes in our notebooks. Usually John says either he wants to live in an igloo with a movie star, or he wants to marry an older woman.

I always say nobody. I won't marry anybody. Not unless we have a house with two doors and two floors, which is not an option in MASH so I don't say anything.

Then usually the teacher hiccuped. She clapped her hands and we did some exercise, like Shakespeare. Or I am in a box and it's getting smaller, or pantomiming animals. When it was my turn, I never knew where my eyes went. I never remember what I'm looking at, I just do it and afterwards I come back into my body. I'm glad drama was just a year. Next year is music, which means you talk even less.

I went over to Mr. Green's last night and he was wearing a belt buckle I'd never seen before. Mr. Green usually dresses nice, meaning not like a man who sits around and reads all day, which is what it seems like he does. He wears jewel colors and not a lot of patterns. His style is soft but with shape. The only other place I've seen colors like that is at church during Advent, so I always half-expect hugging him to smell like incense. When I was little, Mom would say the purple candles are for waiting, and pink is for hope. Anyway, this buckle looked like a cowboy's belt. It had turquoise in it and red stones too, like circles of blood weeping out from Mr. Green's waist.

Is it a big day? I said and yeah, he said, it's my birthday. Every year on my birthday I read a poem and eat some cake. Do you want to do that with me, kid? Okay, I said, and I wished I'd worn something prettier. Or that I'd known so I could've written him a card. Usually I am better in writing. I want to tell him how grateful I am to come over and sit on his porch all the time, and that he talks to me like an adult even when I don't know what I'm doing.

My dad is nice, I love him and not just because I am supposed to. But sometimes when he tells me to calm it down, I see he's worried that I am different. If I'm different, then I'm either his responsibility or a threat. I am grateful for his love, but it doesn't let me be my own person. My dad would never ask me about dates like Mr. Green does. He doesn't even know I had one with Louise.

Mr. Green went into the back room, and when he came out he was wearing a thin blue scarf with gold threaded through it, like sun fingers. I never saw that before, either. My grandma called those sparkle-plentys, I told him. The clothing you wear to feel special. I like that, he said. That's something you do need a word for. Then he made a joke about sun fingers like chicken fingers, and we talked about what you would dip them in. How they would taste. Maybe like dust, Mr. Green said. Dust or coins. Some people eat money, kid.

Then I sat down at the table and he played jazz he likes. It's Mingus. You say it hard on the ming, like a bell sounding. Before I met Mr. Green, I did not know you could whistle jazz, but yes you can. He picks one instrument and just sings it, which is nice because it lets you imagine all the others. It puts half the noise inside your head and half out. When Mr. Green sat back down, he had the scarf tied around his head, and he was holding a cake.

It was a beautiful cake. Pale blue icing, thick-powdered with something glimmery but hard, like if the whites of your eyes were seashells. It looked like a summer other people had, one with lawn chairs and sun hats and toddlers building castles. Summer of strawberries and mint and lovely mothers, standing near oceans with wind brushing their hair. It was not a summer where I had to work at a bookstore, as much as I like the bookstore, most days. Sometimes food seems like it time-traveled to get to you.

There were two squirrel-eye-sized holes in the top where candles must've been before Mr. Green took them out. The cake was chocolate, real but not heavy. We didn't sing. He just halved it and cut one half in two, gave us each a quarter and took the rest back to the kitchen. It was the quietest birthday ever. I wasn't sure if he wanted it that way, or if he was just lonely. I worry about what people really want. This, I guess, is my greatest fear: being so weird that I am alone, except on birthdays when I eat cake with the nut from next door.

I used to have nightmares about it when I was little. Bad dreams about me in a rocking chair facing a white wall, going back and forth and back until my brain just stopped. I started imagining a dog into the room, so that I'd see him and wake myself up before I died. This is really delicious cake, Mr. Green, I said, and he said, isn't it? They always do such a good job. I wondered if he knew he was going to share it with me when he bought it.

When Mr. Green finished his slice, the plate was mirror-clean, though I never saw him scrape any icing. Now it is time for the poem, he said, and I felt somber because clearly he does this every year, and maybe nobody else has done it with him. Here is the poem, he said, and he took it out of his pocket. In my beginning is my end, it started.

I read a line and then he did, the paper open between our cake plates on the clean table. Me then him then me then him, and that's what felt like singing happy birthday. I wonder if it's fair to read a poem aloud when you haven't heard the writer's voice. When you hear someone's voice, you can tell how good they are at listening. At the end of the poem, Mr. Green clapped me on the back like a man and said thanks for spending my birthday with me, kid. I'm going to turn off the sprinklers, and then I'm going to read awhile okay? And I said okay, happy birthday Mr. Green.

I let myself out and walked home across the street, where Mom was making tuna piles for dinner. There are trees in Mr. Green's front yard and there is a nest in one, though I've never seen the bird. I think about that a lot. How if you are a bird, your nest is home. Absolutely everything else is the world. You stick out a wing, and there you are in the world.

People who came into the bookstore today: Two girls in matching whiskery earrings who said their names were Mitten and Queen. A boy in a trench coat who asked for the comics section because he is learning to draw crouching. A woman wearing too much pine tree perfume. She wanted something sad for reading on the treadmill. If you keep walking while you're reading, she said, it won't stick in your heart. A man wondering if I knew the book where nuns made boys kneel on bags of marbles for punishment. A little boy with a neon green military print backpack. On the back it said MY NAME IS, but he hadn't written in his name yet. In the stroller, his sister drew stars on a piece of paper but they were starfish, not stars in the sky. Then she learned how A's are like H's just with rounded tops, so she drew a bunch and her face looked like riding a roller coaster: A A A A A A A A A

Sometimes when I'm reading on my break I imagine polka dots filling up the margins, then going off the page and surrounding me like a blizzard that gets bigger. They hum and make a loud wall of color. I think if I could write everything down important parts will start to pulse.

After I've been under the florescent lights a full shift it's hard to sleep, but it's hard to focus too. So I find a book and read it like a cat watching a mousehole. Something will come. You just have to wait.

One part I remember about Grandma is her dollhouse. Mom isn't attached to it, so I'm not sure where it came from. The walls were all green, crimson, and gold, so inside it always seemed like a holiday. There was one navy room upstairs with a cradle, only the baby was lost, so when I played house I said either she just died, or her mother was in the hospital in labor.

I didn't have anyone to play with so I decided I was a ghost. I wrote notes and stuck them under the chairs, scratched MOTHER MARGARET on the tiny mirror in nail polish with a bobby pin. I haunted the house. One day I decided hell was underneath, so I spent all afternoon making flames out of construction paper and glitter glue and all this red yarn I found. When Grandma came to get me for dinner, she looked frustrated, took it all down and said, this isn't that kind of house, honey. Grandpa heard her and put his newspaper up close to his face, like always when he's about to laugh but doesn't want to make her mad.

Charlene says storytime has to last forty-five minutes, which is stupid because it's hard to get more than eight kids to sit still that long. Plus, corporate doesn't always send very long stories. I get angry looking at the moms treating the book like TV, scrolling their phones while the CD talks. If they aren't interested, how do they expect their kids to be? You have to set an example once you have kids. Maybe that's part of why I don't want any.

When there are more than eight kids and the CD runs short, it's my job to run and get paper and crayons for a craft, which feels dumb sometimes, because shouldn't we try talking about the story together instead? Last week was about an alligator who went to space. He had a helmet shaped like a hot dog so his jaws would fit, and his tail was encased in silver. One boy drew the sky, with planets that looked like chocolate candy, and called it STAIRY STAIRY NIGHT. One girl drew her puppy floating above the moon. Neither picture had anything to do with the alligator, but I didn't know how to help.

Yesterday was another long, slow day. It was almost an hour and a half before anyone came back to music, so I promised myself I could read after setting up the new country music display. If I don't make promises, I just read. I know that about myself. The display announced this lady's third album. Her first was her breakout, her second like robots on ice, chrome and turquoise gleam, and this, her third, was the natural one. Corporate sent a life-sized cutout of her, in soft, glowing makeup and loose hair. Natural doesn't mean no makeup. It took me forever to figure out attaching the stand to her butt.

Anyway, after she got set up I started reading a book about stained glass. In medieval times people made the colors from berries and blood, and then they watched those windows instead of television. I used to want to live in medieval times because the silhouettes are so strange. Pointy hats and veils, and pinched-looking shoes. Then I realized only rich people got those. Most everyone else walked around eating meat and covered in feces. So now I look at those pictures and think about how it smelled.

I wonder if you'd get used to it though, smelling it every day. I think I would, but I think it would make me a different person. This is why I started reading about stained glass. Little bits of blood dripped in hot glass just smells like heat. Reading it made me realize I haven't gotten my period since the show.

Halfway through the book a lady came back looking for opera. I always recommend *Carmen* because it's Mr. Green's favorite and I like that name. It means song, and charm. I'm not going to worry that I'm pregnant yet.

I've had church every Sunday since we've had Sundays. Mom said when she misses her family she finds them at church, and someday I will do the same. She always makes us stay until the very end, when the priest gives a special blessing. On Easter I always wore those lace gloves that snag when you stroke the pew, and the heavyweight white tights whose crotch always sank to the knees. Those tights were the first time I really hated my body, and people telling me what I should put on it. Mom says if I don't wear lipstick, and mauves and golds to match my skin and hair, then it means I don't love myself like I deserve. It's like those people who leave church early. They take the bread and wine and run. Why waste a blessing? I don't know. I didn't feel blessed with my crotch at my knees.

When I was too little to pay attention to the homily, I would imagine flying around the ceiling, or being able to walk on it. There are these big white lights that look like the three-legged tables they put in pizzas so the center holds. When Mom said church was a refuge, I imagined something evil happened outside and we didn't know because we are safe here.

Or else there'd be a fire at home, and nobody would know because everyone would be at the church. A fire so big the house just turned to light. When we got home everything would be ash and black. Dad would get angry, and Mom would hug him and look at me, say not now honey, let's set an example, and then we would hold hands and go live at the motel for a while. We would pretend it was okay, and we'd say it so much it would be. We would eat pancakes and powdered eggs every morning, and I'd have to buy all-new clothes.

No girl who ever actually went to Catholic school dresses like a nun on Halloween, but lots of boys dress like priests. Those boys are always the horniest at parties. Once, right after his parents broke up, John was a priest. It embarrassed me so I decided to protect him instead of yelling. He drank a lot of whiskey that night too, and after a while he sat under the kitchen table. He laid down and said he wouldn't come out until someone gave him a kiss. John ended up falling asleep down there, working it out, so meanwhile I put somebody's sweatshirt over his shoulders.

John and I saw June for fries and then we went to his basement, where we sat on the red beanbag and watched the computer. It is a large beanbag and a tiny screen, so John puts it on his lap and I put my head on his shoulder. I like it because that way we see almost exactly the same the whole time.

Generally I worry about looking stupid, but not around John and so, I don't know: how do you decide to kiss someone? I feel like it's like diving into a pool. I guess some people grow flippers basically immediately, but my first time I swallowed so much water and almost burned out my nostrils with the chlorine. Then I never wanted back in ever, but eventually I tried again and it felt like light.

In the water it's like you don't have a body, which must be how it feels to be close to God. I think that must be how it felt for Mary, except for when she gave birth. Otherwise, didn't she feel sad that she never had sex, ever? Or did she and Joseph have it later? I always thought no. Joseph never seemed like a patient man. He almost walked away from everything. I would have been scared to sleep with him after all that. I would've wanted a vacation alone instead, though maybe Mary didn't have that as an option.

Sometimes, with my head on John's shoulder, I think I should kiss him and see how my stomach feels afterwards. A test. Then at least I could stop feeling terrible and wondering. Finally I said John, when you kissed Rosie, what did it feel like? Pretty soft, he said. Soft like putting on chapstick only over your whole mouth at once. Her hair was long enough to get in my ears. Weird I said, and we kept watching the screen.

Tonight I decided, how would it feel if I was John and kissed Rosie? I put on all the clothes I have that look like his. My dark green shirt with the soft V, and my boxy jeans. The gray velour jacket, even though it's too warm for it. I put on the deodorant John left here one time, the aqua diamond label, and I looked at myself with one foot forwards in the mirror. That's how they say men stand. Only John doesn't stand like that. I looked into my eyes a long time and still had no idea what he'd tell me.

I am bad at math, so Mom made me go to tutoring after school. Sometimes I just couldn't face it so I sat and drew pictures of horses and men instead, or googly-eyed dogs and fat bears all around the numbers. Alternatively I'd go in back and sit by the owner's kid. He was three years old and could recognize cars by their grills. He liked squatting in the window, greeting each one by name. Learning cars from him seemed way more useful than eight times eight. It's easier to look that up if you need to. Plus it made him so happy.

One rainy afternoon I found this soldier guy in my pocket. It belonged to Jay Logic. Jay also had these huge warts, like he was in a fable and a cat sneezed on his hands. Nobody would touch him during the Our Father or share his soldiers, except me because I wanted to be a boy too. We were playing Martian War at recess, and when it started raining I put the soldier in my pocket so its face wouldn't smear.

Anyway, I remember that day was rainy, and Mom came in to sign the parental release. She saw me on the windowsill with the kid, laughing at cars. The Xerox in front of me said seven times eight equals a picture of a rocketship and four times two equals butterflies, and Mom said I didn't have to go to tutoring anymore.

In class next day Danny raised his hand, which looked like half-chewed Juicy Fruit under the florescent lights. It was a stupid question but he asked it bravely, like when Vanessa said what are whippets, or Ignatius announced he was a poet. It wasn't really a question but it had the same feel.

What I want to know, asked Danny, what I want to know is how the penis gets up there. Does it just kind of shlup? He made a sucking noise like getting the last part of the milkshake, and everyone laughed. I wanted to erase time and tell Danny he could have asked me on the soccer fields after class. I really didn't know much about sex, but at least I could say there weren't magnets involved.

This morning, a prepared-looking woman in a leather jacket dropped her father off at the bookstore. I just wanted to let you know, said the lady, which actually means I have made a decision. You might not agree with it but oh well, my job is more important than yours. That's my father over there by the maps, she said. I need to leave him here for a couple hours while I go to this meeting. He should be okay. I'm sure he will I said, because what else was I supposed to do?

He slept in the chair for about an hour, and when he woke up he started thumbing through the stack of books she'd made him, the one I was probably going to have to re-shelve when he left. I felt sorry for him, so I came by to ask if he needed any more books. His voice was like a movie star's. When his body matched it, I bet he went on dates all the time. I hoped that lady knew how attractive her father was.

When he looked at me, I saw he thought I was a boy. He didn't wink or touch my hand, and he seemed like the kind of guy who would do that to a girl. It made me feel safe. It's easier, pretending to be someone else, because you are never wrong if you make it all up. I don't know, he said, but I'm not getting very many thumps from these. This is why I love working in a bookstore. If I said that kind of thing in class I'd get the eyeball, but in a bookstore he's exactly right.

Well sir, I don't know, I said. What gives you thumps? I don't want to read about people who are different, he said. I want books to help me remember. Books like photographs. When he said photographs his lip jumped, and I saw blue gums and crummy spit in the corner of his mouth. I got angry at his daughter, like how I get angry at mothers during storytime. Do you get thumps ever, son? he asked me, and the boy he thought I was said yes.

Yes, I said, especially when I read about the history of the United States of America. A boy after my own heart, he said, it's good to remember where we came from. Please bring me a book like that? Too much poetry here, all these people thinking they have different ways to say the same thing. This terrible need to see each other as they really are. It's a waste. John's mom would tell this man the real waste is thinking you are the only person in the world. Ignoring difference is selfish, she says. I mean, thank god everyone's not my mess. That's a blessing. When she said it she was drinking blush, which is heart-colored wine with bubbles.

I'll be right back I said, in the same tone I used for John's mom. I found him two books with glossy brown covers by white men in suits about white men with ponytails, but when I came back he'd drifted off to sleep again. I put them on the table and left to sweep out children's. If he pees on that chair while he's sleeping in it, Charlene will pitch a fit.

I was waiting for the bus when a big breezy-looking turquoise car pulled up to the curb. Whenever that happens, a car pulling up, I look away. Either it's someone kissing before they go to work or it's somebody looking at me, and either way I don't want to see. At the bus stop, mostly I just want to be reading. I would put a hood over my face, but then I'd never see the bus coming.

This time though, it was Mr. Green. Where did you get that car? I said. I've never seen it at your house. He said it was his girlfriend's. I've never seen your girlfriend either, I said, and he said shut up kid, get in.

We drove down Grape, past the fake Italian restaurant where they give you extra soup to take home, past the bar John's mom says smells like hot car seats, past where you get on the freeway to go to her salon. Mr. Green didn't say where we were going, and that was fine. I was glad to see him, and John wasn't off work for a couple hours. We pulled into a parking lot where I knew Rosie had sex once. It was long and empty. I think once there was a grocery store here but not anymore.

Mr. Green turned off the radio. Kid, he said, get out of the car and get in where I'm sitting. I did, figuring he wanted me to flip the lights, gun the engine or something, while he fixed something under the hood. Instead he unbuckled his seatbelt and slipped over the middle section, so he was sitting in the passenger's seat. That's the first time I realized Mr. Green had a body. He got stuck a little, hiking himself up and over, and I didn't want to touch him, but I didn't want to be unhelpful either. I thought about when he was younger. How moving must have been easier. Then I wondered about his girlfriend, and why she had a turquoise car. By that time Mr. Green was buckled back up.

I got in the driver's seat. Kid, you worry too much, Mr. Green said. I mean, maybe that's the wrong word but your brain's always doing double time and thing is, he said. Thing is, right now you really do need to learn to drive. I will I said, it'll be fine. My parents are just having a hard time letting me go. And I only get lessons once every three weeks. Mr. Green gave me a long look. Well kid, he said, it's up to you. I know you know how to do this, and so I'm just going to sit here and talk until you do, alright? Do you know how to work the mirror?

No, I said. Well look, he said. Here's how it goes. There's the mirror. Look in it. Can you see behind you? Nope, I said. Well move it until you can, he said. That's it. The only wrong way to do it is not doing it. I couldn't tell if he was mad or just being direct. I moved the rearview mirror, and I moved the side mirrors too. I started to sweat and wished I'd worn black today. Pretty soon there'll be circles under my arms.

Alright kid, said Mr. Green. I'm just going to tell you stories while you drive, okay? Don't talk unless you want to. If you want to, great. His hands looked relaxed. I was a little mad at him for telling me not to talk but also, it was nice. Permission is nice.

Mr. Green's dad was a judge, and on Saturdays he'd be in the office until one o'clock when he came home, picked up the turkey and cheese Mr. Green's mom left on the counter, piled the kids into the car, and drove everyone to a movie. Mr.

Green's mom never went along. It was her time and also, that meant Mr. Green's dad could take the kids to see anything he wanted. Usually it was a murder mystery, or sexy. Mr. Green said sometimes they sped to get there on time, but if the cops came, they never arrested his dad because of where he worked.

Mr. Green's dad sounds really good. When he taught his kids to swim, he gave them each a pair of goggles and said, lie on your stomachs on the dock. Face in the water. Look until you're not afraid anymore. After that, said Mr. Green, it was easy just to hop in and paddle. The lake's not that deep anyway, kid. As you know.

When he was little, Mr. Green said, he and the neighborhood boys and Sheena, the one girl, they would half of them stand on one side of the street and half of them the other. When a car came down the drive, they'd fake playing tug-o-war. The car would slow down, thinking it was about to drive into a rope, and the kids would laugh. I wish I'd recorded that, said Mr. Green. The brakes, the laughing, the driver cussing us out. Just the sounds, he said. Not the picture. We weren't cute.

By then I'd driven two clean loops around the park, the police station, the diner, and back. Nothing bad had happened. I wasn't even thinking about bad things. We'll do a few more days like this, okay kid? said Mr. Green. Then you'll be ready for the test. Okay I said, letting the rest go. Thank you, Mr. Green.

Every year they have a Fourth of July party at the punk house. Last year, I was the first one there and I opened the refrigerator. It looked like a flag because of all the blue and red jello shots. I don't like jello shots for the same reasons I don't like keg stands. You look vulnerable when you take them. You show everyone your neck.

This year John picked me up in the car so we had a quick way to get home. We watched the show, and I watched everyone else too. There was a girl in an orange halter top whose back looked like a cage. I wondered if she was hungry or if that's just how her body is.

After the set, which was two guys in jeans and no T-shirts drumming until they sweated through their jeans, we decided to get chocolate frosties and go home. That night we heard they set off fireworks and one of the boys set himself on fire. There wasn't a picture in the paper, but it said his shoulder was bad and also, his opposite hand. He grabbed his crotch so it wouldn't burn. I thought about him in the ER, smelling like sweat and jello and in so much pain. Dad said it was a shame, but I don't know. I could see why someone would think fire was better than day after day after day. I mean, I wouldn't do it myself, but I understand the feeling.

Last night I dreamt I was babysitting three little kids with blonde hair. I dreamt I knew details about their lives, only I forgot them when I woke up. One of them bit me on the neck.

There is a high thin white noise buzzing around the back table in the break room at Chapters. The first time I heard it, I ducked like a fly went into my ear and I moved to the front table, where I couldn't hear the whine anymore. That's good, because otherwise it would be too loud to read. Only that back table has the nicest plant on it, and a big calm painting of a girl wearing yellow and green and leading a sheep. I keep forgetting, try to sit there, and get shocked like a dog. I'm too embarrassed to ask whether anyone else hears it.

When I was thirteen, we got to stay in a hotel for my aunt's wedding, and Mom and I rode the elevator up after dinner. I remember it was red and spiraled gold with tiles on the floor, and they were piping in music. It felt very fancy. I didn't recognize the song, but I knew the shape of it, where it was. Like someone shining a light down from a ship. I felt it in my stomach. Mom said it was a song she'd played for me on headphones when she was pregnant. I asked her if she ever wanted more than one kid, and she said no, just you.

Over by the park, John and Rosie and I got stoned and hot-glued fun meal toys to the benches. Usually I think that kind of thing is just dumb, but Rosie found good ones so it was art. There was a little man with a moon for a head and a sunshine yellow Nudie suit, baby-fist-sized peppermint candies, and these funny red clumpy things that looked like theatre curtains.

We stacked them into towers and glued them on, not where people might sit but along arm or head rests. Like building snow forts, just with plastic. Usually I am scared when I'm stoned, because the weed makes me feel like my body is about to separate into a million puzzle pieces and I can't possibly find them all again. Today was okay though. I kept moving. The only sounds were cicadas, and somewhere, a little kid hollering for his mom.

We went by the abandoned house on our way home, after using all the toys except the hamburger with eyeballs, which looked too scary for public. Rumors go a girl was raped there. To me this sounds like something boys say to be cool, or moms say so you come home. If it had actually happened, some other girl would have burned the house down by now.

Before Rosie's dad made money and built them a new house, they lived in a root-beer-colored shotgun just south of the baseball diamond. Rosie's mom always kept it very clean. One night, Rosie swears a person came in and sat on the corner of her bed. I swear I heard it creak, she told me. Oh my god. She wanted to open her eyes but something told her not to, so she didn't. It's scary, she says. When I try to imagine the ghost's face I can't. It's just a hole. It's hyperspace. She couldn't even tell if it had caused badness or suffered it, but to be that scary without a face is really something. Rosie and John were still together then, so his mom came over with sage to burn in the corners and the ghost never came back.

I think about the ghost Rosie saw, every time we go into the abandoned house. I think if something that terrible had happened, there would definitely be ghosts, though I don't know whose bodies they would have. Maybe something so awful makes its own ghost. A line turning into a triangle.

Just inside the door is the kitchen, which has peach tile stamped with blue roosters, all streaked with ashes, stubs, and broken forties from parties people had. There is nothing on the walls. The curtains must have been ripped down. Now there are just spiderwebs in the corners, silky-trickly and studded with hair and cotton puffs. The drawers are all looted. Candle stubs everywhere like fat dwarves.

The basement is dark, and flooded so bad it looks like a big oily block of ice you could walk on if you wanted to. I was too scared to touch it, because what if her hand popped out? The hand of the girl I never believed was there in the first place.

We planned to microwave a pizza and watch television, only I guess some kid barfed on the skeeball so John had to stay late and clean. I hoped he was wearing gloves. Starlite is so old, by now it all smells like sweaty candy and old milk. It gets in your skin no matter what you do.

I gave up on waiting for John to call, so I just bused over and let myself in using the leopard-print key his mom keeps in a code box under the porch. She used to keep it under a rock, but one day somebody took it and let themselves in. They didn't take anything but they left a flashlight in one of the beds, which John's mom said scared the shit out of me guys. The sheets were glowing and I couldn't tell whether there was a body or not too.

John's mom was home already, eating buttered crackers with one hand and kneading her foot with the other. She had one big black ring around each eye, from rubbing. I know what kind of mascara she uses, because John gets his from her. It comes in a black tube with feather loops on the cap. She had a glass of wine mostly gone, and then I was glad that kid vomited, because when John sees his mom like this he gets really sad, and I can't do anything about it. Hi I said, and she said hi, honey. It's good to see you.

I love John's mom. She's honest about being tired, even when it makes John worry. Sometimes when Dad comes home his face looks like that too, like shadowy dough, and he sits at the kitchen table and Mom rubs his shoulders a minute. He never rubs her shoulders. They don't talk. It's like work never gets easier, and they're just waiting it out. Waiting for me to go. I don't know what they'd do if they had different jobs, though John's mom could do anything. Normally I hate television shopping, but even I would buy something from her. I'd buy her crystals or emergency packs, or clocks shaped like fish. She could be the face of a fragrance.

How did it go today? I asked and she said it was fine, honey. Same old. Do you ever get bored? I asked and she said sweetheart, John's father used to say having an adventure is a sign of incompetence. I am incompetent here at home, not at work. Then she blinked, like she hadn't realized it was true before saying so.

You are not, I said, and she said look lady, I'm eating crackers for dinner and I'll be asleep when John gets home.

But that's okay, I said, and poured her some water. She stood to drink it, which was good because that meant she was about to go to bed.

Do you know why we got divorced? she asked, her hand quivering a little around the glass so I knew she was actually pretty drunk. I never met John's dad, but they married Catholic so divorce is a really big deal. Divorce is like you gave up. You can never marry anyone else, even if you fall in better love, or if your first partner hit you or stole. You don't have to tell me, I said. I don't think you messed up.

She put the glass down. Well honey, she said, he was older and honey, I knew he was going to die first. In the beginning, that was comforting because I'd have time to myself. But, she said, and then her face looked sober, I really actually started to believe how a Catholic does. I realized that time alone in-between wasn't even a heartbeat, in eternity.

I realized, John's mom said, that forever was serious and he was a terrible father. Can you imagine, just sitting there in that big sparkly room with him forever? With the angels? And time doesn't even matter anymore? I hate it when people say they can't even imagine something, so I said I could imagine it and yes, that sounds terrible.

Now John's mom was swaying, gripping the back of the chair to hold herself up, so I decided to treat her like a customer. Do you need anything else before you go to bed? I asked, and she said no, sweetheart. But do you understand what I mean? I do, I said, and I meant it. He must've been a terrible father. I knew you would, she said, and she went up the stairs and I heard the bedroom door close, not the bathroom one, so I knew John's mom was safe. The bedroom door closes softer because it goes over carpet, not vinyl.

It was a relief John wasn't home yet. It gave me time to make cinnamon toast the way he likes it. Enough butter to melt the toast on top, then sugar in its own layer, then cinnamon. Half the time he comes home he thinks his mom left it out for him, but half the time it's me. I like John's mom's butter knife. The handle is pearlescent, and if you run hot water over the blade it cuts the butter easier. It was probably a wedding present.

When I go to shows I see why Mom loves church. She hates that I say that, because she doesn't think different kinds of places are holy. There's just one, and that's the point. But why feel guilty about anyplace that's home?

I could chart what makes shows and church the same. Incense and dirt, chorus and refrain, blood and blood. One guy we always see out, his hair is starting to gray like silver whispering. He has these scars in his cheeks from when he'd put safety pins through and pull down on them. There are plenty of scars in church too, in people's foreheads or hands. In both cases it's because someone believed in something strongly.

Mom doesn't talk about my hair, which I know she feels is generous. She thought it was because I wanted to stand out as an individual. But that's exactly what I don't want. I just think my hair should be purple. When I close my eyes and imagine my face in a mirror, I see purple. I read a book where a girl's hair grew pink, and my favorite part was nobody told her it was weird. They only wanted to know what made it pink. It's always been this way, she told them.

Ever since I messed up with Louise, we've been avoiding the diner. John's starting to get annoyed. He likes those fries best, so I promised we could go back as soon as I bumped into her someplace else. Finally we saw her last night at the punk house. The band was a guitar, drums, and a girl playing death maracas, which are glass jars filled with shards of glass. When that drummer came out, he rolled his right pant leg to the knee, and he took off his glasses and put them in a pouch with the extra sticks. Then he just squinted at everyone.

The band played in the middle of the living room instead of a corner, and halfway through, the drummer got polka-dot drops on his shoulders. At first I thought he was sweating weird, but then I realized it was spray from everyone dancing. There was a girl with violet lipstick standing right in front of the kit, and when his hi-hat smashed her hair wafted up from her shoulders.

Louise was dancing too, her hands, and she had on this red top that looked like a square from a television show that taught kids about shapes. Instead of trying to make eye contact with her I just nodded at John, to make sure he saw her too. Finally he mouthed YES OKAY, and then I realized he'd been kind, waiting patiently to go back for fries and June.

The band played one set and then pizza came. I wanted some but didn't take any because kids at the punk house are weird about who pays for food. Once I came straight off work and hadn't eaten since noon, and I would've gone cross-eyed without a slice of cheese. So I ate one. This girl got really mad, and so did I because I know her dad pays for everything anyway. The trick is to look at the shoes. See if they're nice. Hers were real leather, the color of a roasted turkey, and if she has those, she can pay for pizza. Anyway, after everyone ate, the band played another set, and by then I was so tired John and I just fell asleep, crisscrossed on the couch. One hand was on my purse and the other around his ankle. There was a lady in the corner, stoned and eating meringues someone made. She said they were the colors of all the people in the world.

I dreamed that the cupboards in the kitchen were refrigerators filled with food. When I woke up, I saw yellow and realized someone had put a blanket around my shoulders. I thought it might've been Louise but I didn't know for sure. My mouth felt like greasy water in a rain gutter. I found some mouthwash in the bathroom, spat it out in the bathtub, and woke up John. We drove home without talking.

It was five o'clock, enough time to sleep a few hours for real before work, or to lie down and watch the light happen. Mom was up when I got in, drinking black coffee at the kitchen table in her bathrobe. Your father and I were talking, she said. Are you in love? Is that's what's going on? No Mom, I said. Well, maybe. But right now I'm sleepy. Okay, she said. Just checking in. Good night.

Walking home after work, right near the doughnut kiosk I saw a funeral procession. All those cars with their headlights on and plastic baby's breath and roses, probably the kind with fake glue raindrops, taped to the roofs. I wondered if you leave those flowers in the graveyard too, and who gets to be in the front of a funeral procession. I've been to funerals, but never for anyone I loved, so I wouldn't know for sure. I would have to get someone else to drive anyway. The emotion would make me weave.

Usually when a procession goes by, people walk outside and stand on all the porches with their hats off, but today I guess everyone was busy. I did the Sign of the Cross when the first car came by. There were about fifteen of them, and a little girl was in the back of one. She had a stuffed monkey and was looking out the window solemnly, like she wasn't sad but had been told to be quiet.

I guess I looked sad too, because the woman who runs the kiosk, we buy maple bars from her sometimes on Sundays even though they're too sweet, she came out and hugged my face into her breasts. I think she thought I was crying. She smelled like lavender and Crisco, and her shampoo. The woman said she hoped I had a boyfriend, because he would take care of me when I got home. I said yes, me too. Thank you. She held me until all the cars went by and the policeman in the rear turned the corner.

Last Sunday I woke up before Mom, and I went to church on my own. She always goes at eleven and sits in front, but if I go at nine I can sit anywhere I want. I like going on my own because there's nobody watching. I can sit in the back and listen, and figure out what everything means to me. Remember, Mr. Green said when I started crying about that yard with the tiny white crosses, crying about the babies, your God doesn't have to be exactly like their God. You just have to sit next to each other sometimes. Mr. Green said you know something matters if you keep coming back to it.

I like sitting in the back pews with sun across my face. It's magic when it comes through the stained glass because those colors are so saturated. They don't reflect anything. It's a love that's just there. It's like sitting with John at the diner. He never ever says I love you, but sometimes he puts cream in my coffee and takes the first sip to make sure it tastes okay.

Last Sunday it was raining outside. This place is an old church with a wood roof, so there were a couple buckets in the aisles to catch leaks. There was a little brother I recognized from storytime, sitting a couple rows ahead and listening for the plops. He kept splaying his fingers and looking at them like he was surprised. I wished I had a flashlight to shine so he could make puppets, though he was probably too small to keep paying attention.

Halfway through the homily, the boy spilled his cup of dry cereal and started crying, so his mom hiked him up on her hip and walked towards one of the stations of the cross on the wall. They are wood too, like the roof and the pews, and the people are made of burns not ink. Some parts are painted. Jesus's eyes look like dark coins. The one where the mom stopped had him in the crown of thorns, with a gash in his side. The blood was the same color as the cherries on the boy's bib. See? said his mom. See, that's Jesus.

The boy made an a-ha noise and kicked his feet hard, like how babies do when they're excited but can't say so. Watching him, I realized I'd missed the homily. I turned back around and started watching Father's hands. I guess I wasn't supposed to get communion because I slept with the drummer, but I wanted it, and I didn't want to feel badly about sex either. When I went up I bowed before I took the bread, my knees stiff like bending into a pool of water.

When I graduate I have to go away, because otherwise I'll just take care of everyone else. My head will get full, and I'll start thinking about stories and people as facts, as statues or set, and then I'll get tired eyes like John's mom. Mr. Green has this calendar with buffalo on it. They look soft and stubborn. Rocks wrapped in brown carpet. If you stay, he told me, you will look like buffalo. If I stay, my brain will be full with people I don't want to be like. Sometimes it already feels like a clown car in there. It's getting so full of customers, shows, and rules I'm worried it will tip over and I'll fade. When I see people here sitting on their porches in white tank tops holding a beer, looking out without speaking, I think of cars on their sides.

Today we drove up and down Grape about eleven times. Mr. Green said this routine is going to make me fall asleep kid, and it did. Asleep, his face lost the wrinkle I thought was a regular part of his forehead. His breathing sounded different, but it wasn't snoring. I imagined Mr. Green was a paint-by-numbers page and decided I would color his shirt purple.

He was out good so I pulled into the grocery store lot, parked and pushed back my seat. I wanted to think. I know he keeps a notebook in his glove compartment, for writing down lists or directions. The cover is gold if gold had a layer of dust on it, and it is all blank because he rips pages out before he writes on them. Those notebooks are all over his house too.

So I got it out, and wrote down all the words I could see from where we were sitting, in that lot with its flags red like shouting and poor trees choked by concrete. Kinds of gas and pop, animals for sale, teller open. Respect life. I wish I was a photographer because then I would remember today specifically, just from that minute of looking around. When you take a picture and someone else looks at it, it's like John and I watching movies together. It's different than reading the same book.

Mr. Green's eyes were still closed, and I felt lonely and also creepy for parking at a grocery store when I didn't want to buy anything, I just wanted to sit. I tore out the page, revved the engine up again and started looping back along Grape. If he's still asleep after two more laps, I'll turn on the radio and that'll wake him up.

Mr. Green likes reading magazines. He leaves them all over the backseat. Sleek ones, the kind with headlines about dresses at awards, or diminishing birth weights, or plane crashes. Science fiction ones too, and art magazines with people shaved naked. Everything was new to me. I never saw anything we got in at the bookstore.

One was about a skiing accident in the mountains. I guess this guy lost an eye, and his wife was killed. He spent the insurance collection on a miniature of her. The magazine said her name was Karen. Karen's miniature was perfect. It had her green eyes and her pale, lavender-blonde hair, and her feet were posed right. Heel to instep, like they make you do for First Communion photos.

Then this widower, he put miniature Karen into a miniature snow globe, and then he put the snow globe into his empty eye socket. He said true love meant more than any fake or patch. I asked Mr. Green if that really happened, and he said what do you think, kid? I kept thinking about the widower at the grocery store, buying half the food he used to buy for two. The cashier would say are you doing okay, sir? and the widower would nod. The snow would swirl around.

I took the bus to work the day the guy went crazy in magazines. I got there at eight-thirty, not eight, so Charlene gave me the stink-eye from cookbooks, which is where she shelves when she's mad. But whatever, Charlene gets paid more than I do, and she's not in high school like I am. One day I'm going to leave, and she won't. It's just a bookstore. One day I'm going to go or they'll tell me to go, and it'll be okay.

For the first half hour it's a ghost town. Everyone is up front, pawing through calendars and magazines and paperweights, ordering complicated coffee. Except this one guy Leo, who has curly strawberry-gold hair. Leo usually comes back first, because he knows I'll just let him sit. I'll just let him read. Charlene wouldn't. Leo calls me Girlie.

Once Leo got through a whole fine dining cookbook in a day and a half. Once he smelled like shinguards and small, wet gems. Once he said he lives at Jesus Saves! on Smart and Pike, where they kick you out plus breakfast sandwich at seven-thirty. If you don't have meetings you're supposed to be with your kids, and if you don't have kids you're supposed to be job hunting or at the VA. Leo just comes here and reads, which is fine.

We don't talk a lot. It's like we go to the same gym and ride bikes at the same time every day. Sometimes when people fret over sale price or where is your classical or something, Leo and I will look at each other. He will roll his eyes, and I will make the face like a fish hook caught your lip. Neither of us is supposed to be here this much.

The day the guy went crazy was a first of the month, so we were switching up the racks. I spent forty-five minutes fighting a cardboard mobile and fifteen stickering explicit stickers on the wrong albums. Twenty more doing it right. A lady came in and wanted music for morning walks, this guy wanted a song for a wedding dance with his mom. I did one sweep for stolen merch and nodded hey to Leo, who was chewing his finger and reading about musicals.

I was late because last night John and I fought. We were going to meet at the wall in the park, but he didn't come for two hours and he wasn't answering his phone, so I walked to his house and sat on the stoop. I didn't just let myself in because I wanted him to know this was important. When he finally came home I said John, I am not a mope but if you say we're meeting somewhere, it's mean not to show up. He looked at me like my face was an Etch-a-Sketch and he could shake it. Point is, I said, point is I love you John. Then he really got mad. I didn't know what to do, but I'd already decided I wouldn't let him make me feel dumb.

By then I'd really missed the last bus, so I told Mom I was at a friend's and slept on John's pull-out couch. He was still mad. I dreamed weirdness, like it was the Rapture and I had some of John's hair so he had to find me. He rode a big yellow bike, and afterwards I helped him find his tooth in the lake too. Next morning I got up and left before anyone was up. I sweat a lot when we fight, so I smelled terrible. The bus from John's is an hour away from the bookstore, and that's why I was late.

Pretty soon Steve came back so I could go on break. I wish Steve was my cousin so we could hang out on Christmas. I gave him my name tag and my swipe card, and I went in the back. Don't go over, okay? Steve said. Storytime's in an hour. Steve, I said. Steve, don't worry I know. I couldn't tell if he was worried or just wanted to say something. Sometimes I think our name tags should be two-sided. One is our name for the customers, and the other is a list of things our co-workers can talk with us about. Mine would say Joan of Arc, house shows, and where are the best doughnuts.

I don't eat in the lunchroom because it's depressing. Last week the lady from biography went on about giving birth. I didn't ask either, she just started. I guess she was in labor one whole day, and ate only wild strawberry gelatin and chocolate pudding and ice chips. She said it feels like you are inside a ring of fire. I said that sounds terrible.

Instead I go in to grab one of those magazines missing a cover, then take it to the parking lot to read about makeup. Sometimes I rip out a perfume sample and keep it in my pocket. Today's sandwich was second day from the coffeeshop. Limp pink bacon, rubber ball cheddar, and chicken like soft cheese, an orange sauce over everything. I ate it while reading about DIY saddle shoes. The trick, if you want wingtips, is an X-acto knife.

The thing I didn't tell John is that I am maybe pregnant now. I mean, maybe not. But maybe. I'm one week over four weeks and also, I never asked the drummer's name. I told myself if it goes five more days, I am going to buy a test. It is helpful, when you are sort of scared, to set a date when you should be really scared. Before that it's fine. I want to tell John, but also I don't. It complicates everything. Also I wish it was him instead of me. Him wondering. He probably wouldn't even go to work.

When I got back, Leo was reading an opera and Steve was reading at the register. You aren't really supposed to do that, but Steve's been here longer than anyone else, so he can. It's storytime, I said. Duh he said, and we got out that week's costume.

That day was a cat in a hat and blue check jacket. He had round brown cheeks and potholder paws, and one eyebrow looked off. I took Steve's elbow and we walked out together. He sat down and I pressed play on the CD. It was warm in the store and suddenly it felt like I ate glue instead of a sandwich. Maybe if I am pregnant I shouldn't eat cheese that bright. I started thinking about how John's neck smells. How he taps his teeth when he's thinking. Sometimes we watch shows and his fingernail is louder than the TV.

The CD read a while. The cat sings in a band. He eats jam and butter sandwiches. After he made friends with firemen, I saw Charlene running down the center aisle, fists to her chest. Leo came four steps after her with his galoshes walk, stopping quick to re-shelve the opera book. I thought, whoa. I squeezed Steve's shoulder twice, which is our sign for I am coming back, and I went to see.

There was already a small crowd. The man wasn't anyone I knew. He had a muscle-smooth body, khaki slacks and a polo shirt and he was crouched a bit, like a defensive line was coming. First I saw his eyes, which looked like those ping-pong balls they grab on TV for lotto numbers. All the man's muscles were lit up. A small map of sweat was spreading across his chest. First it was a phone booth, and then a farm town. His body was all different parts of things that aren't bodies. I couldn't see him anymore.

Charlene talked to the crowd and then to the man, like his freakout meant he couldn't hear anyone else but her. Has he moved at all? she said, and then in the same voice sir, can you move? I was learning about Charlene. She would go down with the store before the rest of us.

The man was statue-still except for the sweat and his left hand, which quivered. Leo was behind me. That's not going to do any good, he said, looking at Charlene, and no kidding I said, though I didn't know what would. I wondered if the man needed medicine or a vacation. I felt something wrong was happening, but that doesn't mean knowing how to fix it.

The man was holding a copy of *American Pet*. It had koi on the front so I knew it was the new issue. The old one was puppies. The magazine was in the hand that was shaking so its pages kept whacking together, and a subscription card loose-winged to the floor. Maybe we just need to get that fish thing out of his hand, said Leo, like now we are all on a team. Maybe that's what he needs.

Leo stepped up. Hey man, hey he said. Hey man, you're okay. He told the guy what he was going to do, and then he started doing it. Leo was going to keep walking and then he was going to take the magazine, and after that we'd all put it back on the shelf together. Do you maybe want some water first, man? Okay, here we go. Leo reached for the magazine and it slipped out fine after one tug. The guy's eyes didn't change. I thought I heard his teeth. Charlene threw up her hands and went in back to call someone.

Then I remembered I was working and looked around, instead of at the man. There were no children. It was mostly teenagers and moms who'd left their kids at storytime, or moms who didn't have kids at home anymore. They wore jeweltones and had smile lines. There were a couple men in from the offices across the street. Usually they come for meditation magazines or financial papers, or meetings in the coffeeshop with girls. Most of the men looked frightened, like they'd seen themselves in a mirror with a mask on. Some looked like they were writing a story inside their heads. I realized Leo left somewhere and then I remembered Steve, stuck in a cat costume across the store. I hustled back to rescue him.

Guiding Steve back through summer reading, I saw men coming in with a stretcher. When we finished the costume change everyone was gone, tumbleweeds. Everything back to the same. Soon it was half an hour until I was off, and my head felt like it had fog stuck inside it. I sold chocolate to a lady in a headscarf. Cartoon soundtracks to a girl who paid in quarters. I think these other girls stole some jazz discs too, but who cares.

The bus home was quiet. The seats on it are brown with flecks of pink and green and sometimes gold. When I was little I thought if you got one with gold you were lucky. At home I put my keys in the dish and went straight upstairs.

I peeled off all my clothes and laid them out like another me lying on the floor. The shower was hot and I sat on the floor, closed my eyes until I was worried I'd fall asleep. Then I washed, trying to see if anything felt different. If anything hurt or was rounder. I decided to wait three days to tell John, then two more and we'd buy the test together. If I couldn't find the drummer, maybe John and I could move in together. I thought about that man at work. I wondered if he'd had breakfast. Would his family find out what happened? Did he have a family he could call on the phone?

Afterwards I toweled off a little but not a lot, and not my hair. Then I went into my room and closed the door. I stood in front of my desk and put up my arms and just spun around, my hair whipping out and little pricks of water all over everything. It wasn't a plan, it just happened.

I spun and spun like a sprinkler, like faster, like when you're drunk and lie down and the bed feels like a boat. I spun like I'd see blood or a bruise if I fell. Like if the curtains were open, the neighbors would see me naked and think I was crazy. Then I fell into bed and went to sleep.

Dear John,
When I think about where I live after school, I can't see anything but not here. And I don't watch movies with anybody else so I want you to come too. I felt weirder not telling you

Dear John,
It's worse if I never say anything, so

Dear John,
Maybe this is dumb but otherwise I freeze

Dear John,

This guy came into work today. His friend died, and he wanted to get a tattoo of a fist with dirt in it. The drawing he made looks like a punch of earth. Punch worms and earth into your teeth. Punch you with death, not into it. He wanted a drawing like that in a book but we couldn't find one.

Dear John,

I keep trying to start this letter and not finishing it

Dear John,

Let me finish okay? I think home is love so

Dear John,

Last night at dinner suddenly Dad said he wants to be cremated then flung out over water. I don't know what water. We were eating meatloaf. I guess he can do whatever he wants but it was weird he said it so frankly. He said he brought it up casually so it didn't seem scary but I knew it was already a fact. It was not casual. I bet he and Mom talked about it a lot beforehand. Mom says she isn't sure what she wants to do. She likes the idea of being cremated but when she misses Grandma it's nice to go to a gravesite. This made me think about myself after they die and then I thought

home
death
what

DON'T WRITE ABOUT DEATH!

Dear John,

Hey,

Dear John,
I keep trying

John likes working at Starlite Jams on summer Fridays because it's so weird. On Fridays, the Catholic Youth Organization Summer Camp asks kids to bring in three dollars for lunch. One pays for the lunch, and the other two go to the food pantry, which Rosie says has more shelves of cheddar fish crackers than she's ever seen in her life. The lunch is always chicken soup in styrofoam. Salty with noodles like white gelatin pencils, and chicken smell but no visible meat, and one piece of bread for dunking. It's not supposed to fill you up. The idea is it gives you empathy for hungry people. I think this is dumb, because how can you help anybody else when you're hungry? When I went to camp I hated it.

But John says actually it's pretty funny. Those kids' parents still drop them off at Starlite on Friday nights, only instead of spending quarters on skeeball, the campers buy ice cream cones or hot dogs, or too much pizza. He said one kid today, he was so hungry after nothing but that stupid soup all day that he asked for two hot dogs in one bun. It's funny but it's dumb too, says John, because they end up wasting more. When he said it I realized it would have been okay just to bring a granola bar or something, on fast days, but I never thought to do it. I just felt my face turn into a cave.

The other thing about Friday nights are the bulimic girls. Rosie used to throw up sometimes too, so I kind of understand. Her thing was she liked the fish sandwiches but she hated corporations, so she'd eat a triple with tartar sauce then throw it up like a fuck you. She would enjoy it, but she wouldn't let herself keep the energy because that was the other thing, Rosie said. Waking up next morning feeling strong, and hating herself. I don't need that, she said. I refuse to spend their energy. If I didn't vomit I would lose the whole day.

When they were dating, John thought it was all really punk. Sometimes he wouldn't even make her pay for the sandwiches. At the time, I thought it was so sweet. He knew what she wanted, and he gave it to her. John said tonight we went through like twice as much pizza as usual, and I said that's hilarious.

Yesterday John's mom was happy after work. We came over and she had macaroni and cheese all ready. She uses the yellow boxed kind, but she cuts in hot dogs and puts paprika on top, for a bit more color. The macaroni Mom makes is all white. It looks frightened. John's mom talked about being pregnant, but not like the woman at the bookstore did. Like she'd spent nine months walking through the desert to meet John, and when she met him she was so happy. You were a real sweetheart she said, and John looked down into his bowl. I read somewhere that when you were in my stomach my blood sounded like a vacuum cleaner running. So when you cried, we'd put you next to the vacuum cleaner, and then you fell right asleep.

It was funny, hearing her say we like she was two people then. I don't even know what John's dad looks like, though John's hair and his mom's are different colors, so that gives me an idea. I thought about the time I found a condom in the garbage can in Mom and Dad's bathroom, which was good because it means they have sex for fun, not just to have me.

When I was born, John's mom said, my parents didn't know if I was going to be a boy or a girl so I had two names waiting for me. I was almost Michael she said, and laughed. But then science got better so we knew you were going to be John. Even then though, she said, I kept calling you Zeke because that was my little brother's name. And until I met you John, he was the only baby I knew very well. You even scrunched your faces the same way. But pretty soon you were John.

Dear John,
What if we went away? If we ate less pie senior year
I bet we could go somewhere after graduating. You

Dear John,
Do you want to go

Dear John,
My brain is hamster wheeling so I need to tell you.
Sometimes that cinnamon toast

Dear John,
I want to go away with you so you know you can go

DON'T BE HIS DAD

Dear John,
I love my parents, they're weird but they found each
other, and Mr. Green and even Rosie when she's sad,
and talking to your mom when she gets home and
eating food together. When I was little I worked so
nothing ever changed. I tried to breathe in rhythms,
and I made sure all the lights were off when I left a
room. I couldn't fall asleep if the door was closed
because it was too quiet and nobody else could ever
come in. And I like being alone to read, but John,

I don't know
Maybe there's no spark

UNGRATEFUL

Dear John,

How do you know where you're supposed to leave? I think I'm supposed to want to be in a city, because there I can be anonymous or I can meet people exactly like me. But that seems tricky, like if you're not all working towards something you could cancel each other out. Sometimes I think instead I'd like to go somewhere tropical. Someplace full of flowers, just coming up in-between people standing around. Let's go somewhere nothing's familiar

Dear John,

After the bookstore I have no idea how I'll make money. But I'm not worried

Today Mrs. Johnson came in to buy some books for her sons, who are eight and ten and like mysteries, or books about geography. Once, a couple summers ago, Mr. Johnson hit Mrs. Johnson in the mouth and she called Mom from the closet, crying. I answered the phone and she sounded curled a little at the edges. Like paper too wet to lie flat. I guess as soon as he hit her she ran in the closet, and her sons ran out into the street. It's hard, said Mom, that they ran opposite ways. I wonder if any cars drove down the cul-de-sac and saw those two boys at the end of the driveway. I would just watch the house, wait for its walls to turn invisible so I could see my parents inside, talking it out.

Next week in church Mrs. Johnson had a raw eye, but they stayed together said Mom. She looked at me then said, I guess that's best, if they have kids. I don't know. I tried to imagine why you'd hit somebody you loved. I thought about hitting John, like making a fist and actually hitting him in the face, or something he could do that would make me want to hurt him, and I couldn't. When I see Mrs. Johnson in the store and ask her if she's had a good day, I really want to know.

I went over to Mr. Green's for coffee and peppermint patties. We sat outside and he started talking about his friend Phil, who died twenty years ago. Both of my best friends from when I was a kid died, said Mr. Green, and I said oh that's terrible. I'm sorry. I imagined John and Rosie dying, and then I felt too far away to say anything more.

We were really young said Mr. Green, but I always loved Phil. I used to try and copy his handwriting, so if I ever had to pretend to be him I could. Mr. Green said Phil had cancer. The kind you get from the sun. Phil didn't get it checked out until it was too late. For the longest time afterwards, said Mr. Green, everything just felt really loud. I unplugged the phone at night, I didn't play music, and I didn't watch basketball on television. And then one time, he said, he fell asleep on the couch. On a hot night, like breathing vegetable broth. He dreamed the phone rang and he answered it, and it was Phil.

I was just so relieved to see him alive, you know, kid? said Mr. Green, and I said yes, because I could imagine it. It was just such a relief to see him back, physically I mean, and talking to me. Losing your friends is like lights going off in a city. I could tell by how Mr. Green sounded that he didn't believe he'd imagined Phil. He believed Phil really was talking to him. That story is what I think grace is, said Mr. Green, and I nodded and ate more candy.

What I know about other people's bodies / KEEP THIS DON'T FORGET:

- John has a freckle in the center of his kneecap and a short list of people who are allowed to touch his head. When he is interested in something small, his entire body compacts. He crouches towards it on its level.

- Rosie has a knob behind her left eye. If it was bigger she couldn't wear sunglasses because the stems wouldn't fit. Last summer it got big and her dad said to check it out, but then it drained so she didn't and now it's back again.

- Mr. Green's joints pop and his spine is moon-shaped. He doesn't have feeling in some of his fingers because he got frostbite when he was drunk and didn't get warm in time. He holds pens with three fingers in a point, like smoking a joint.

- When John's mom is listening to you, she knots her fingers in her hair and slides them up and down at right angles, like drawing a tic-tac-toe board.

- Mom has a polio vaccine scar on her upper right arm. It looks like someone pushed half a bristly hairbrush into wet sand. When I was little I'd see it when she couldn't put on her suit jacket until the deodorant dried.

- Dad dries his underarm hair with a blowdryer. I never saw him do it but Mom said so.

- Charlene eats bagels the same one way: rip in half, bite one end, start talking at me. Chew. She always gets plain flavor and so everything smashed in her mouth is one color.

In eighth grade religion they gave us all dove-blue booklets with the gospels in them side-by-side, so we could see where Matthew, Mark, Luke, and John contradict each other. Well, not contradict exactly, said Ms. Taylor, more like enter into conversation. Mutually illuminate. My favorite part was the list of miracles and parables, because lists always seem true. They save you from worrying about forgetting. The booklet was small enough to slip into the front covers of our Bibles.

Next they gave us spring-colored markers to highlight the parts that are the same and the parts that are different. In the end there isn't a lot that's the same. It's like those four guys are little kids telling about their dreams, this and this and then this, I mean eventually everyone will say everything, but sometimes there's a cliff. Sometimes time leapfrogs, or turns into lace. Sometimes in church when Father says things have always been this way, I want to whack him with that dove-blue booklet. Nothing has, not even the stars.

Yesterday I left work after going an hour overtime, because the new guy slept through his alarm. Charlene looked frustrated but she has to look frustrated, plus the new guy looks like a teen magazine model so she'll just fake yell at him. She only ever really yells at girls. It's days like this I can't wait to leave.

My brain felt like sparklers so I decided to walk home, past the empty lot that makes Rosie feel guilty because it has this big billboard with an alien-bud baby connected to an old man in a wheelchair. It is about how they both deserve to live. There isn't even a mother in the picture. Once Rosie spit at it. Over by the dumpster I saw a gray lump I thought must be a sweatshirt. Then I realized it was quivering. It was a cat. I got closer and started saying hi sweetheart, hi but she didn't react to my voice or shadow.

She was shaking like sitting in a bowl someone else was shaking, crouched right in the middle of the sidewalk like an announcement. One eye gone and the other closed, and her face was covered in oozy milky threads, dripping off in a tangle. It looked like a veil I could take off for her. It looked like something a person in a band could perform, only this was a real cat. I was scared to touch her because if that stuff shouldn't be on her body, it definitely shouldn't be on mine.

I'll come back honey, I said, it's okay honey, which wasn't a lie because I believed both outcomes even if I didn't know how. Sometimes you say that stuff and it really means I Am On Your Team Today. And I was. I walked to the chicken place two blocks down and said I need to use your phone, there is a sick cat outside, and the guy looked crabby but he let me do it.

I dialed Animal Care Control and said there is a sick cat outside, and the lady said calm down. How do you know? She listened to me like I was a child and she was in charge of an army. She's on the sidewalk and doesn't recognize anything, I told her. Okay honey she said, we get lots of calls but we'll see what we can do.

I hung up and the man behind the counter made me buy a soda at least, kid. I thought he was being mean. Obviously the cat wasn't code for anything. It was a real cat. I never saw her again so just threw the soda in a trashcan without drinking any, and walked the rest of the way home.

Dear John,
Remember when we wanted to be archaeologists and Royalty died? We buried her by the onion in your backyard and made that calendar and waited a month. Then we dug her back up and she still looked like a cat. I'm sorry

Dear John,
Mom really believes people who kill themselves go to hell. What?! It's like telling a story about a person and I can't see his eyes. How do you believe something nobody on earth can ever really prove is true? Nobody ever proved hell. Nobody ever even proved guilt. I mean okay, I guess maybe but why hold onto something if it hurts? That sounds like an excuse. I would cut my guilt out of my chest

Dear John,

I know God is not a buffet line, but I don't think he would threaten me with forgiveness, I mean really we need to be forgiven for what

can you be forgiven if you never felt shame

every time you die you get a new sense, one we couldn't even think of before, and pretty soon we can't even think of ourselves

could I find him
maybe it wouldn't matter

Dear John,

Remember when everyone thought that tornado was coming through, and the sky went that pickle-juice-purple color, and I started praying to Mary for protection? It was weird, I didn't think about it I just started praying

Dear John,
Praying I don't

Dear John,
If God takes you out of your body

I hadn't seen Rosie in a few weeks so I went to check on her, plus I always tell Mom I'm at her house even when I'm not. Rosie was at the computer and had half a grilled cheese with pimento on the desk. She doesn't like pimento but it makes her eat slowly, which is different than not enough, so I don't give her a hard time about it. Hi she said, without turning around. Did you eat? Yeah, I said even though I hadn't. Eating with Rosie is a lot of work.

She said I am reading about Julian of Norwich again. I said oh god Rosie. But she kept going. Hold up she said, lifting her hand and I saw there were teeth painted on the fingernails. I don't actually know how to get close to Rosie, I just know how to come to her.

Hold up, she said, my favorite part about Julian is she asked Jesus to hurt her so she understood how he felt. How much pain he was in. Okay, I said. I didn't know if Rosie was trying to convert me or catch up or what. Your sandwich must be cold. Whatever, she said. I like them cold.

Seriously, she said, Julian had all these visions and she didn't know how to remember them all or say what they meant. But then Jesus said hey, I kept everything alive in you anyway and now you have a better understanding of it. That's when Julian started writing, said Rosie. She stopped comparing herself to everyone else, and she just wrote.

That's like you, Rosie said, which surprised me because Rosie doesn't think about other people very much. Here, she said, and she gave me the book. Julian wrote it in her abbey, said Rosie, and people think she had just three windows. One to the church so she could hear Mass, one to the servants so she could get food, and one to a porch for visitors. Nuts, right?

Just windows? I said. Yeah, she stayed there the whole time, said Rosie. That's more like you, I said, and she laughed and ate the rest of her sandwich. Rosie, you're so weird I said, and she grinned. Nah, Julian's cool, said Rosie. She didn't have to choose between the convent or marriage. She went straight to God and that's why she scared people. I wasn't totally sure who Rosie was talking about anymore. It's hard to listen to people the right way.

After we were quiet awhile, Rosie said I still feel bad about our baby. But it's not regret it's just like, now I know a ghost. But he was always a ghost. It's not like he was ever going to be a baby. I know, I said. I'm glad you're okay today. Yep, she said. I'm alright. I put my hand on my stomach but I didn't tell her anything. I still have one more day, and besides I'll tell John first.

Last night this girl Carly played at the house. She plays keyboards like a waterfall, and when I hear her I forget what time it is. It was really humid, so they killed all the lights and gave the people up front candles to hold. Carly has bad stage fright, so for each show she pays two or three friends in beer to wear these figure skating costumes she found in the free bin at the thrift store. They wear ski masks too, and paint the tips of their hair like rainbow sherbet. She gives her friends instruments with rubber bands for strings, and everyone dances around her while she plays. It is a lot of work to stay calm, but you do what you have to do. At first I worried the spangles would catch in the candles, but that didn't happen.

Afterwards I sat on the porch and wished I had a cigarette so I didn't feel strange sitting alone. Sometimes I want people to talk to me, and sometimes I don't. That night I just wanted to look. At work I'd read how in medieval times people knew where they were by holding mirrors face-up in their hand and looking at the stars. This makes more sense than pointing at a map. When I was twelve and slouched, Mom said imagine there is a string in the middle of your head connecting to the stars. It's kind of the same thing.

This guy came out and sat next to me. He said he was Ian, and was I lonely? This is a dumb question because yes, duh. To dodge it I said what do you do? and Ian said a month or so ago, he and his friends built a nest in the parking lot of the grocery store. It was pretty funny he said. People brought over cereal to donate, and one girl just took a nap while her mom shopped. It was, he said, an expression of community and solidarity and I said that sounds dumb, you already have homes.

But then I felt badly, so I said I mean you do, don't you? Ian said yes. I hadn't offended him. Then John came out and put his arm around me, which is code too. He's checking in. He waits for me to say something, and then he'll pretend he's either my brother or my boyfriend. I forget how we worked it out, but we've done it a long time. Last night I just looked over and said let's go home.

What bothers me most about those crosses in the yard is how white they are. They are just white. Selfish. They are for the babies, not the mothers. Rosie is-was a mother, like I wouldn't buy her a card saying it, but she is a mother. Her body said yes, I can do this. I can start to do it.

The worst part is those crosses are that terrible bleached white, not starlight or cool white, which say maybe color is coming. Bleached white is just like, no story, which of course is most threatening of all. It would at least be funny, and truer, if some were red. Sometimes I imagine those crosses in boxes in that family's garage, stacked and labeled next to the holiday decorations. I'd never forget to lock the door.

On break at work I read about classifying gemstones by color. If it's purple, it's amethyst and always will be, however it is possible to heat sapphires to clear. I dreamed that I saw all these colors but couldn't describe them, which made them secrets. I dreamed some grew from trees like fruit. Some glowed in rock. They were jewels, but they weren't hard. You could squeeze them to drink. Diamonds looked greasy but sapphire was sour, and let in light like mouthwash does. When I drank one it made my throat clench, but I liked it. Afterwards I imagined my guts sparkly. Nothing in the dream was new. This was always how it was.

There was a lava river going through there too, in my dream. Warm and alive, but fragile like hearts beating underneath. Its color dulled crimson-purple at the edges, but bleated pink in the center where it was boiling. Lizard-things skated on the surface of the lake, sometimes leaving three-second footprints that looked like toed leaves. I watched the surface for hours, tracking colors not bodies. I wanted to show John, but he wasn't around.

Before I left to come back home I put a gem in each pocket so my hips and chest were glowing and I could see forward in the dark. I don't think John's brain makes pictures like this and I don't think he'd even want to talk about mine, which is where the difference is. You don't have to be the same, but you can't ignore why not. You have to be on a team, not just bored in the same ways.

I didn't see Leo for a few weeks, but then he came back with someone who must be his friend. Leo's friend said hello to me specifically, which meant Leo told him about me, because otherwise he would have said hello to Charlene too. She was looming at the entrance, highlighting something in green on a pad. We are here to read, said Leo's friend. We won't fall asleep. I said that's cool, I didn't think you would. He had squares of tinfoil in his pocket and his breath smelled a little like whiskey but not too much, so it was okay. I used to build rocket ships he said, and I said that sounds amazing.

They picked out one book together, and sat down on the blue couch where that kid puked. If people ask I tell them to sit somewhere else, but if they've already sat I don't say anything. At this point it's probably clean. You shouldn't really ever sit down on upholstery in a public bookstore anyway. If you care about that stuff. The two men shared the book, resting the spine where their legs met, and Leo's friend read aloud. He asked for help with the hard words, and after he got tired Leo took over. It was nice, listening to them.

Rosie surprised us and actually got a job. She drew all the produce signs at the grocery store. An apple core near a snake. Strawberry shortcake, melons. She was best at seeds and ice cream topping. For a few weeks Rosie seemed happier, sunnier, but then she got that look. The look where you are missing your leg all of a sudden, and nobody knows but you. You know you can't move forwards but everyone else just thinks you're slow.

Eventually she started running in the afternoons after work. Sometimes she'd run again at night. Sometimes I saw Rosie running down the train tracks, elbows poking out, like stamping triangles on the hem of a dress. She got thinner.

Then she got her second job, which was at the bakery, the one that makes the bread for Communion too. We used to get excited about it, eating sandwiches there. It was holy just with ham. Her shifts were early in the morning so she could take off in the middle of the afternoon. John and I started seeing her at shows more often, but she didn't always say hi. She stopped answering her phone, and I stopped just coming over because she had a different schedule now, and I didn't want to run into her dad. I figured she'd let me know when she wanted company, like always.

We started talking at the bakery though, just small things like how is the weather. Once I came in for a cinnamon roll and Rosie had out a pocket mirror and was drawing blue half-moons under her eye. Her lips were pale as salt. It's fucked up, Rosie said, but you get better tips if you look tired but pretty. Yeah that is fucked up, I said, because I didn't know what else to say. What the hell. It wasn't even Halloween.

Rosie said she'd saved enough for a bus ticket to New York. She was going. It was weird, I didn't even know she was thinking about it, but she was and now she is gone. Now her mom is the one who looks tired. I haven't seen Rosie's dad in weeks.

The new guy at the bakery is very religious. When I came through the TV was playing preseason football, and he said he'd never be a quarterback. He could never get that close to a dude.

Dear John,

That professor came back into the bookstore today. I don't think he lives nearby. He buys magazines with men on the covers. Strong men, with muscles like balloons. The professor says he puts his kids to bed every night. He kisses his wife, and then he drives over here where his office is, and he writes about philosophy and then he sleeps a little. Next day he wakes at five o'clock and drives home to make his kids eggs. At first I felt sad about that but today I was thinking, what if this guy and his wife have a deal? What if she likes it? He seems cool. Sometimes

when people say they don't want to judge, they
really mean they're ignoring you

Dear John,
Write what you know, okay, but I DON'T KNOW

Dear John,
I want to live with someone I love

Dear John,
I don't want to live

Dear John,
You can make all the choices about the house
I just want my own room
My own room with a door
Dear John,
When we're sitting at the din

Dear John,
When I talk to you

with you

Dear John,

BE CLEAR

At the grocery store all of a sudden, this lady took my hand. She had on all these bracelets and charms and nail polish, everything clickclickclicked. She said honey, right now we are all just bulbs in the chilly ground under rocks, waiting for Jesus to come back. There are tendrils waking up inside of us. I thought maybe she needed a pop, but then I remembered dreaming we were all in church and our chests cracked open, and green shot out. The ceiling was a garden or a jungle, all buzzing.

You don't know what seed's inside until it grows, she said. It could be flowers or coconut or corn. I told John and he said you're a weird one sometimes, you know? How do these people find you? But then he squeezed my elbow.

Dear John,

In confession Father asked the closest I ever felt to God. I lied, because the real time was when Rosie got that acid and we biked in circles and I saw music pouring in white through the window. Remember we fell asleep? I dreamed I didn't need a body anymore. We were skeletons looking down at ourselves, pink and yellow blooming in our chests

Dear John,

It's easy to talk to Mr. Green because I know exactly what our relationship is

Dear John,
All I really need when we move is access to a library. Not a bookstore because then we'll need extra money.

Dear John,
Remember that ark they painted on the side of the gym? The entrance was also the door to the ark. The dads painted the animals on Volunteer Day, so some had lumpy eyes and most looked like bad dogs. Inside in PE, when it rained I pretended you and I were the last people on earth

Dear John,
Today this woman came in and was like, it's my daughter's birthday tomorrow. She wants to be a writer. She is trying to find her voice. I think that trying to find her voice is the stupidest. She already has one, just maybe she's not saying what you want. Speaking isn't about purity also what, purity

Dear John,
Remember being little, and that playground before they took the sheet metal merry-go-round away? That mean kid with the windbreaker asked how we wanted to die. It wasn't a threat, it was fortune-telling. I forget what you said, but I remember mine because he laughed at me. I said I wanted

to die slowly because I was scared of my brain
disappearing and the kid said that is so stupid.

Dear John,
I don't want to be a buffalo

I need to move

Dear John,
If I'm pregnant we have to

I don't know how to find that guy, and even if

Dear John,
How can we save money when

John,
The crazy thing is I think maybe
Is it crazy if

I'm not scared about the actual birth because by
then it has to come out
DON'T CALL BABIES IT
I'm scared about not being able to put my hands
down in my lap
I like sleeping on my back

Dear John,
Seriously how did you and Rosie know you had a
spark?

Dear John,
How do you start?

Dear John,
Okay so I guess the other way I could go out on dates
with people I don't care about. Mom says those are
practice relationships but that seems worse, it seems
like giving your own self a swirly

Dear John,
What I worry about most is what if when I die, I turn
into two people or maybe three or four. Everything
won't be in one place
Dear John,
Stop protecting me

Dear John,
If I put everything I own in boxes, it would be two
boxes

Dear John,
Is it selfish to move when things aren't necessarily
bad?

I know how to be old here

Dear John,
It's not selfish

Dear John,
I could throw up

Dear John,

GOD

Dear John,
I used to dream about flying almost every night. Mom liked asking did you have another flying dream. She had them all the time when she was little too. I like thinking we inherit dreams, not in the hopeful corny way but in like, our minds are the same. I wonder if you share dreams if you share a bed with someone long enough. In my flying dreams I remember I was always really happy. My arms were always out and my chest curved into a C, like a proud little seal

Dear John,
Last night I dreamed I was the mom and Mom was me

Dear John,
In a dream you're everyone in the dream

Dear John,
Mr. Green says never let someone who doesn't love
you take your picture

I woke up in the middle of the night and it felt like my teeth
were in my stomach not my mouth. There was blood on the
sheets. Soaked through to the mattress. Not a scary amount,
but enough to feel like I'd had a bike accident. Some of it was
darker. Jelly-lumps. I peeled off the sheets and drank milk
while I waited for the water to turn warm. Then I scrubbed
the sheets and filled the bucket and put it in my closet to soak.
Tomorrow I'll slip them in the dryer before everyone else
comes home. Mom wouldn't care, but Dad would. He doesn't
see change, so he'd just think I was sick.

I'm pretty sure I'm not sick. I never did tell anyone about
maybe having a baby, so now it's like it never happened. By
then the sky was light orange. I took two aspirin and fell
asleep, wrapped in my quilt on the dry side of the mattress.

Today a woman came in wearing black jeans coated in shine.
Her hair was sleek too, like how you can stroke the back of a
cat's neck with a finger and it will purr. I love working at the
desk because everyone who comes up will talk to you, and it
will be about something specific they need for their lives.

Honey, she said, honey I need a book about how to keep plants strong. Okay I said, well there are different kinds of plants. What kinds of plants do you have? I don't even know sweetheart, she said, and it was mostly okay she was calling me sweetheart because I think she meant you are a nice, smart person who will help me. Sometimes customers call you sweetheart and it means can I have your phone number. I don't even know, she said, except everything is green. Nothing has a brown trunk or needles or anything.

Okay I said, and we started walking towards gardening because even if you have no idea what's going on it's still helpful, walking next to someone. Do you know why I need plant information? she said, and I noticed her eyeliner was crazy steady, like professional makeup artist good. No, I said, and she said well I trust you so I'll tell you. See I have a lot of stress in my life honey, she said, and so sometimes I drink, and at some point I started stealing plants. Oh, I said. From planters by the university she said, or people's yards, or just down here along the main road I guess. I don't remember doing it, but I see them in my bedroom when I wake, and of course there is dirt on my dresses and underneath my nails sometimes. That's how I know it's me.

I wanted to ask her why her friends let her do that, but then I realized I should probably just be listening. I wanted to ask why she wanted books on gardening and not addiction, but that definitely seemed like a bad idea. I like drinking, she said, especially gin with bitters. It tastes like echo. I looked at her to see if she was drunk right now. I didn't think she was, but everyone's different so you can never be sure. Maybe she was a real poet instead.

I saw a psychic, she continued, about what it means when you want more green in your life and the psychic said I am trying to return to the garden. The Garden of Eden, she said, and she looked at me like maybe I hadn't heard of it. I sighed and said yes well, here we are in your section. Thank you sweetheart, she said, and then I went back to the desk.

Dear John,

Today this dad came in, he wanted tips for reading books to his daughter. He wanted steps and he wanted titles. If they are actually books about boys he said, that's okay because I will just change the pronouns. I said no. Don't teach your daughter to lie. She needs to know those books were written by someone who didn't know about her. That doesn't mean she can't love them. Charlene gave me the stinkeye, and the guy left without buying anything.

Dear John,

Sometimes I wish I was already dead because if I wrote in medieval times, I would know everyone who would be reading my books. I would know all their names and addresses and I would see them in the square every day. I would be like yep Frances read my book, but I still have to get eggs from her

Dear John,
I went to church again this morning and I forgot
my body while Father was talking, but once I left
I didn't know how to believe in everything he said.
Everything in the church. He said our hearts are like
geodes, you have to crack them open and see. But
what if your husband hits you, what if your kid dies?
Kids die.

Dear John,
Magic is not the way to understand everything,
christ

splitting
MAKE IT ABOUT YOU

Dear John,
We have to make our problems into something
interesting

I don't know

Dear John,
Mr. Green says epiphanies are gifts

He says don't mourn a life that wouldn't make you
happy

You can't squeeze a rose I guess

John I love you

Dear John,
If I write it down I'll find out how it ends

ACKNOWLEDGMENTS

Thank you beloved family who helped me finish this book:
Mom and Dad, again and again, and Siobhan, again, and
Bunny, and Stephanie Acosta and Kristi McGuire and
Christy LeMaster and Jessa Crispin, and Jerry Boyle and
Matt Malooly and Rob Leitzell, and Jacqui Shine, Mariapaz
Camargo, Sarah McCarry, Rahawa Haile, Emily Culliton,
Mona Awad, Teresa Carmody, Maggie Queeney, Jacqueline
Pallardy, Sarah Schantz, Lizzie Ehrenhalt, Daph Carr,
Sarah Dodson, Sierra Mitchell, Brit Parks, Caroline Picard,
Elisabeth Baker, Katherine Swan, Mattilda Bernstein-
Sycamore, Hazel Pine, Denise Dooley, Hanna Andrews, Nell
Taylor, Alex Bush, Tina Celona, Melanie Johnson, Christine
Cody, Rachael Olson-Marszewski, Fred Sasaki, Chr*s Estey,
David Lasky, Michael Matos, Ed Marszewski, Toby Carroll,
Tom Comerford, Hanson Dates, Robb Telfer, Mathias
Svalina, Douglas Wolk, Kahlil Smylie, and David González.

Thank you readers and teachers: Matthew Goulish, Patrick
Durgin, David Stuart MacLean, Adam Levin, Beth Nugent,
Britteny Black Rose Kapri, Molly Zuckerman-Hartung, Dana
DeGiulio, Selah Saterstrom, Eleni Sikelianos, Bhanu Kapil, Billy
Tuggle, Ken Van Dyke, Hero, and especially Brian Culhane.
Thank you Steve Tomasula for the light to start, and Chip
Delany for the key to finish. Thank you Bob Glück, Rachel
Levitsky, and J.R. Nelson for solid advice at the right time.

Thank you Doctor Molly for summer. Thank you Jill Summers for the office.

Thank you, thank you Jason Sommer, Naomi Huffman, and Sydni Chiles.

Thank you classrooms, libraries, and lakes inside academia and out, and Skylark, the Hideout, and especially the Nightingale for being home. Thank you, Chicago Chicago Chicago, for teaching me to wear wool and stay in love.

Deacon Bruno, Matt Garber, Charlie Clements, Nicky Rahn, Tito, and Brother Mike: your names in fire, forests, and metal.

Hugest gold letters, love, and fried pickles for Tim Kinsella, and the great Zach Dodson, and Forevertron for Ed Crouse. This is a book because of you. Thank you.

And a lighthouse of opals for Joshua North-Shea. I love you.

NOTES

"Rage like a blood filled egg" is from David Wojnarowicz's *Close to the Knives*.

The book dream is Chris Estey's music dream.

The polka dots are Yayoi Kusama's.

The upside down pineapple upside-down cake is Pat Cashman's.

Lots of gestures here were first recorded (by me, at least) at the shrine on 17th Place and in my 2013 Naropa Summer Writing Program notebook, in particular at lectures by Kazim Ali and Anselm Berrigan.

"In my beginning is my end" is from "East Coker" by T. S. Eliot.

"splitting" and the split house on the cover are references to Gordon Matta-Clark.

"See You in the Morning" is a quote from Jim Woodring about Kenneth Patchen's fourth novel. "See you in the morning," says Woodring, "is an excruciatingly tender, pathetic genius of hope."

Mairead Case is a working writer born in 1983. She also works in high schools, at doors and libraries, and against the prison industrial complex. Mairead finished this book in Colorado, where she is currently an English and Creative Writing Ph.D student at the University of Denver.